no regrets

A NOVEL

Rebecca deMond

This book is a work of fiction.

Names, characters, places, and incidents are a product of the author's imagination or are used fictitiously. Any resemblance to actual persons, living or dead, events, or locales is purely coincidental.

Copyright © 1974-2016 by Helen R. Letts
Cover design by Helen R. Letts

All rights reserved. No part of this book may be reproduced, scanned, or distributed in any printed or electronic form or by any means without the express permission in writing from the author.

ISBN-10: 0-9889333-5-7
ISBN-13: 978-0-9889333-5-4
Printed in the United States

Thanks to Thomas Wardman for his help giving a digital life to some old material and to
Heidi Schmitz for her review and suggested updates

And gratitude and thanks to Patricia Jones and Linda Foreaker Eckman for their enthusiastic and unwavering support

.

no regrets

A NOVEL

CHAPTER 1

It was a Monday morning, the beginning of a new work week, and Samantha Ward wished herself anywhere other than her office at Syntronics, located on the very eastern edge of the city of Bellevue. The fact that it was a day with weather reminiscent of those typical winter days in Washington State, filled with rain and accompanied by the grey and gloomy atmosphere that persisted during that season, had little to do with her desire to be elsewhere. Today someone new, someone other than a Ward, would begin directing the day-to-day operations of the software engineering company her father had founded. Had the person been a stranger, or had the circumstances been different, she might not feel the almost suffocating hostility she did. But, the person was not a stranger, and the circumstances were cloaked in mystery.

Even now she still found it difficult to believe her grandfather, Charles Ward, had betrayed not only her, but also her father, or at least her father's memory. Exactly one week before, just after lunch, her grandfather had strolled casually into her office as he had done so many times during the last six months and made an announcement that threatened her already fragile world. Without preamble, he had informed her he was delivering the management of Syntronics into the hands of an outsider. Except he didn't say "outsider," she did. At the same time, he refused, despite her plaintive cries, to name the successor, but alluded to the fact that it was someone imminently qualified to direct Syntronics and to inject new life into the company.

Her grandfather's refusal to reveal the name of the individual had struck Samantha as highly peculiar because since early childhood he had been exceedingly open and very communicative of her regardless of the subject matter. Distressed by what she considered to be a major deviation in his character, she spent the week trying to persuade him to answer her questions.

The times she had been able to corner him were few; he seemed to make a point of avoiding her. On every occasion she had beseeched him to give her more explicit information, pointing out that she, too, had stock in the company and had every right to know what changes were being made. He consistently stonewalled her, saying she would know soon enough. Finally, on Friday, she learned, along with all the other Syntronics employees, who was taking over. It was the "who" that filled her with resentment.

Before she had even finished reading the memo announcing the arrival of the new manager on Monday, Samantha had flown out of her chair, charged out of her office, and walked as fast as her legs could carry her into the former office of her father, now occupied by her grandfather. She had sped past Carol, who had been her father's administrative assistant for many years, and had flung open the door of the executive suite, ready to vent her anger on her grandfather.

Upon finding the office empty, she had turned back to Carol, her chest heaving as she gasped for air, and had demanded to know where her grandfather was. Carol had stared blankly at Samantha for some seconds before saying, with an apologetic air, "Sam, I thought you knew. At least I thought he would have told you."

"Told me what?" Sam had asked, angrily twisting the memo she still held in her hand into a tight little knot.

"He just left on a trip," Carol had told her.

"Left? On a trip? What trip? Where was he going? How long is he going to be gone? Did he leave the state?" Her mind had been racing with all kinds of questions.

Carol had responded to the barrage of questions with, "He didn't say. He simply told me he was leaving on a trip and that Mr. Sloan would be here Monday morning." She paused, and then added, "Oh, he also told me some workmen would be arriving this afternoon to make some alterations to the executive suite for Mr. Sloan."

This last bit of news momentarily distracted Samantha from her main purpose—that of ferreting out information about her grandfather's whereabouts. "Alterations? What sort of alterations?"

"I haven't the slightest idea, Sam, but I can tell you that I'm positive that your grandfather has sanctioned every move that Mr. Sloan has made this last week."

Carol hesitated a fraction of a minute before offering Sam more details. "Mr. Sloan has been here several times during the week. In fact, he's met with department heads. But mostly, Mr. Sloan has been here evenings. Every night this last week he and your grandfather have been locked away in that office going through your father's records, examining the books, making plans."

Samantha's mouth had clenched tightly shut, astonished to learn that her grandfather had been having secret meetings and had deliberately excluded her from those meetings. She was a department head, too!

"How long ago did my grandfather leave?"

Carol had glanced at her watch. "About 20 minutes ago."

Samantha had given Carol a hasty thank you and had dashed to her car, in hot pursuit of her grandfather. She had raced to his house, which was just minutes from the office, only to be told by his housekeeper that he had left ten minutes before for the airport. All of Sam's questions were met with an "I don't know" by the elderly woman.

Sam went back to car and sat. Feeling frantic and exhausted, she contemplated her next move, and realized that she had none. Her cell phone history showed page after page of calls made to her grandfather. In desperation, she decided to try to reach him one more time. After multiple rings she was about to hang up when her grandfather answered. Her voice raspy from a combination of nervousness and anxiety, Sam hadn't bothered to return her grandfather's greeting, but had asked with an agitated tone. "Granddad, what is going on?"

He had retorted with irritation and disbelief, "Sam? What's wrong?"

"Granddad, where are you going?" she had growled. "Why is Jake Sloan taking over? Why Jake of all people? Why didn't you tell me?"

"Sam," he had cut her off in mid-sentence, speaking more loudly with each word he uttered. "I'm going to miss my flight. I can't talk right now. Good-bye, Sam. I love you."

With a loud click, the conversation had ended. Frustrated and hurt by her grandfather's cold dismissal, she hadn't returned to work. Instead she had gone home and stomped around her townhouse, trying to guess why Jake Sloan had been selected to take over Syntronics. It had occurred to her to call John Simms, head of the programming department, and inquire whether he had been included in the secret meetings with her grandfather and Jake. She abandoned the idea when she realized that making such an inquiry would alert John that she had been excluded.

And here it was, a new Monday. The Monday Jake was to officially start, and she was still pondering the reason why he was at Syntronics and dreading her first meeting with him. She was wondering what would happen, how she would react when they did meet face to face when the sound of high heels clicking down the tiled floor outside her office cut into her thoughts. The sound signified one thing. Karen, Syntronics' very young and very cute receptionist, would be entering her office at any moment.

In preparation, Samantha hastily opened a file lying in the center of her desk, hoping that she would look so totally absorbed in her reading that Karen would take the unspoken hint. The quickly arranged prop didn't work. Karen appeared in the doorway, paused briefly to ensure Sam was the only occupant in the office, and walked in saying breathlessly, "Have you seen him yet?"

"Seen who?" asked Samantha politely, pretending to read. She knew very well who Karen was referring to. For more than seventy-two hours the name had been prominent in her thoughts.

"You know," Karen moaned in a voice mingled with disgust and astonishment. "Him. Jake Sloan." Without waiting for an invitation, Karen seated herself in one of the two available chairs in front of Sam's desk.

"No," Samantha lied, "I haven't seen him." She only wished it were true. She had actually glimpsed a tall, male figure dressed in a suit from behind as she scurried down the hall to the sanctuary of her office an hour previously. There was no question it had been Jake.

"Well, I have," the curly-haired blond boasted with a toss of her head. "He's gorgeous! Big beautiful blue eyes, dark wavy hair that curls slightly around his ears. And what a build. Why I'll bet you..."

"Karen," Samantha said, more sharply than she intended even though she really didn't want to hear another word. She was too well aware that Jake was an extremely handsome man.

"...he can send tingles down a woman's spine" the younger girl said dreamily.

"Karen!" Samantha snapped. "Enough." Recalling that she, too, had once experienced the "tingles" to which Karen referred. The girl's assessment of Jake Sloan was more accurate than she knew.

Looking innocent and wide-eyed, Karen asked, "Was I getting carried away?"

"Carried away?" Sam said sarcastically, closing the file and opening another one stacked on her desk. "I thought you were writing copy for a Jake Sloan fan club."

Giggling, Karen deliberately dropped her voice an octave. "I could you know."

Samantha laughed despite herself. Karen's exuberance could be engaging, but it could also be tiresome, especially when it involved gossip. Except for this one failing, the petite nineteen-year-old Karen was one of the best receptionists the firm had ever hired. Fortunately, Karen exuded only charm and professionalism at the front desk, leaving girlish antics for the inner sanctum of Syntronics.

Samantha tried to change the subject by asking Karen if she had finished adding the new list of customers Sam had given her the week before to the company database. After responding that she had, Karen cheerfully turned the conversation again to the subject of Jake Sloan.

The young girl was uncharacteristically serious when she asked, "Sam, do you think Jake Sloan would be interested in a...well, a...younger woman?"

Not wanting to hurt Karen's feelings, Samantha chose her words carefully.

"Karen, Jake Sloan's interest in companions..."

"Yes," prompted Karen, as she leaned forward in the chair.

There was such eagerness in Karen's eyes that Samantha quickly changed what she had intended to say.

"...is anyone's guess." Samantha wanted to tell Karen that Jake Sloan's sexual preferences were of no interest to her and certainly none of Karen's business. On hearing Karen's next sentence, Samantha regretted not being brutally honest. So much for the soft approach thought Sam.

"I'll bet you're just as curious as I am," Karen speculated, her nose a little higher in the air.

Exasperated, Samantha retorted that she wasn't and decided it was time to bring the conversation to an end. In no uncertain terms, Samantha told Karen that she shouldn't be so interested in the personal life of the firm's new manager. The remark silenced Karen for all of two seconds.

Shrugging a shoulder, Karen replied rather flippantly that Jake Sloan's private life was an open book and reminded Samantha that his picture often appeared online and that each time he was pictured with a different companion.

Frustrated with Karen's "so there" attitude, Samantha threw up her hands in the air and said in a very level tone, "Drop it, Karen. Jake Sloan is a barracuda, who I'm sure has the proverbial little black telephone book and a woman's name for each letter of the alphabet. The very fact that he's seen with a different woman at each social event he attends should tell you what he is. He's a womanizer."

Samantha's vehemence startled Karen. Karen rose hastily from the chair she had been occupying and mumbled something about returning to work. The girl was almost to the door when Samantha called her back.

"One more thing, Karen," Samantha said, "You're too good for the likes of Jake Sloan."

CHAPTER 2

The words were barely out of Samantha's mouth when Jake Sloan appeared in the doorway behind Karen. The firm set of his lips and the slight movement of his jaw told Samantha that he had heard every single word. Well, she thought, it was as her mother used to say, no eavesdropper ever heard any good about himself.

Karen stood transfixed, eyes darting from one to the other, and started like a startled fawn when Jake addressed her. Samantha would have recognized the deep resonance of Jake's voice anywhere.

"You're Karen Simpson, aren't you?" he said smoothly and Samantha smirked and had to muffle the sound that accompanied it. She was sure by now he knew the name, social security number, and vital statistics of every Syntronics employee. Jake was known to pay very close attention to even the most minuscule details of any business he took over.

Karen answered so meekly that Samantha blinked in astonishment. The girl nearly swooned when Jake flashed her the slightly lop-sided smile that one social media blogger, with little originality thought Sam, dubbed "irresistibly wicked." The label hadn't been that far off the mark though. Not only had Jake been blessed with a dazzling smile and sexy voice, he also had the kind of appearance romantic novelists were fond of describing as tall, dark, and handsome. His was a face a sculptor might have shaped, with a high forehead, slender nose, strong cheekbones, and a square chin. He was a man that attracted attention and most generally from the female population.

A blushing Karen replied, "Yes, sir," and made a hasty retreat before he could say anything else. For the second time in an hour, Samantha heard the clicking of high heels against the tiled floor of the corridor. She wanted desperately to call Karen back—to again have some physical barrier between her and Jake. She wasn't prepared to be alone with him.

Jake's husky "Hello, Sam," sent a chill down her spine. Even after more than a decade, he still had an unsettling effect on her. The realization added to the anger that had been building inside her for days.

Samantha returned his greeting with a cold, flat, "Hello."

Jake crossed his arms and braced himself against the door frame. One eyebrow was arched slightly as he gave her a sweeping appraisal. There had been significant changes in her appearance since they had last met one on one. She no longer looked like a schoolgirl, but a beautiful, mature woman of twenty-nine.

Her hair no longer hung to her waist. Now it was brushed away from her face, a tumble of soft curls barely touching her shoulder. A wispy fringe of bangs fell of its own accord just above one eyebrow. In certain light, the rich auburn tresses looked like burnished gold. The oval face was thinner, the freckles were fewer. Samantha's lips were just as shapely and as full; the eyes still a warm hazel. But the mouth was set a little more firmly; the eyes were not as bright with innocence.

Jake's cool assessment ended. "How long has it been, Sam?"

His continued use of her nickname annoyed her. "Not long enough," she answered rudely. Even from a distance she could feel his piercing look. She hoped a defense of rude remarks, stiff retorts, and frosty stares would hasten the end of their meeting.

"Too long," commented Jake, unperturbed by her nasty remark. "I can see that I should have finished what I started twelve years ago."

Samantha went pale remembering the occasion to which he referred. At sixteen she had been mesmerized by Jake's charm, envying the young women whom he escorted to dances and other social functions. Her girlish infatuation lasted until just after her seventeenth birthday, to a night she had never spoken about to anyone. With supreme effort, Sam brushed the memory aside.

"Is there something you want?" she asked belligerently.

Jake's jaw shifted. In answer to her question, he stepped into her office and shut the door firmly. He closed the distance between them with a few short strides of his long legs. She watched his advance through narrowed eyes. When he came to a stance between the two chairs positioned in front of her desk, she loosened her grip on the desk's edge and dropped her hands into her lap. She drew back in alarm when he leaned forward. Barely an inch separated their faces.

His voice was as low as it had been when he had addressed Karen, but the tone was anything but soft.

"I expected you to give me some trouble, Sam. I can see the hostility as well as hear it. Let me give you some advice. Don't even try to do battle with me, Sam," he said. "You'll lose. You, my sweet Sam, will do exactly as I tell you. No questions, no debates, and most assuredly, no arguments. Obedience. That's what I want from you. Understand?"

Samantha's face flushed red with anger, her almond shaped eyes mere slits. Jake's words had the same effect as a needle pricking her skin. The anger that had been mounting since she learned that Jake was taking over Syntronics exploded like an overinflated balloon. She nearly jumped out of her chair.

"You...you ask me if I understand! Understand!" She spat between perfectly even teeth. "No, I don't understand. I don't know exactly what devious means you used to coerce my grandfather into delivering Syntronics into your hands, but I do know they were devious. As far as I'm concerned your association with this firm is temporary and of short, very short, duration."

She was breathing irregularly at the finish, two spots of color marking her cheekbones. In contrast, Jake appeared perfectly relaxed and amused at her outburst. The faint smirk that tugged at his lips rekindled her anger.

"I'll be damned if the son of the man who crippled my father is going to take over the company he founded."

For the briefest of minutes, Jake's face turned a fiery red. He recovered quickly.

"You should be careful about making inflammatory and slanderous statements like that," he warned. "You may have to pay for them later."

"It'll be a cold day in hell," declared Sam hotly.

"Exactly," he said with deadly calm. "It's a day I look forward to."

It wasn't the threat but the steely blue glint in Jake's eyes that silenced Samantha. His chest heaved and his nostrils flared. She recognized the physical manifestations of controlled anger. Though disappointed that she hadn't won the scrimmage, there was a small measure of satisfaction in having gotten under Jake's skin.

Jake was the first to look away. She watched him stroll around the tiny office, scanning the titles of technical books packed tightly into a bookcase, and examining an assortment of diplomas and colorful prints that decorated the walls.

There was no evidence of anger when he faced her again. His eyes were clear, his breathing steady.

"You know, Sam" he said casually, picking up a glass paperweight that held a stack of papers in place, "you can always resign."

Samantha's hands rolled into fists at the suggestion, her fingernails cutting painfully into her palms. She regarded him with a mixture of hate and suspicion.

"That's a ridiculous idea, especially when I own forty percent of this company."

"And I own sixty percent," he informed her bluntly, setting down the paperweight with a loud thud.

If he had slapped her she couldn't have been more shocked.

"You can't," she whispered.

"But I do" he affirmed as Samantha shook her head in disbelief.

"Granddad wouldn't...," started Sam, but she was cut short by Jake's, "He did."

"No. No." The denial was almost a cry. She had refused to believe that her grandfather had actually given Jake a controlling interest in Syntronics. She had assumed that Jake would hold a salaried position and had decided over the weekend that he would hold no power over her. What was she to do now?

Jake was curiously still, his attention held by a beautiful face pinched with pain. Her eyes, now more green than hazel, were glassy, as if tears were not far off.

Occupied with her own thoughts, Samantha was oblivious to Jake's scrutiny, her head bent as she digested the news. He had called her name for perhaps a fourth time when she finally turned her head toward him. She wondered why he was frowning. After all, it was she who had sustained a shock.

"What did you say?" she asked in an expressionless voice.

He repeated his statement. "Be ready to discuss the SALCOMP project at ten a.m. tomorrow. My office." He glanced at his watch, then back at her. "Ten o'clock sharp," he said again. Without waiting for a reply, he left.

CHAPTER 3

Samantha didn't know how long she sat staring into space, mulling over the encounter with Jake. She wasn't going to believe that he had sixty percent of Syntronics until she heard it from her grandfather. Jake had to be lying. She reached for her desktop telephone and dialed her grandfather's number, praying he had returned from his mysterious trip. On the twentieth ring she replaced the receiver with a groan of frustration.

The remainder of the workday Sam spent battling the urge to rush into the executive suite and demand Jake give her a full explanation of his presence at Syntronics. Trying to work was hopeless. She would start to read content for the SALCOMP project, only to lose concentration after just a few paragraphs. Her mind continually wandered back to Jake.

She searched her mind as she had done for several days for a possible reason for her grandfather's actions and came up empty. Knowing the exemplary lives her grandfather and her father had led, she ruled out blackmail and extortion. There was simply no rational explanation.

Anthony Ward, Samantha's father, had started Syntronics

when she was ten years old. A graduate of the University of Washington with a degree in computer science, young Anthony had been ambitious. With a small loan from his engineer father, Charles, Anthony had set up a one-man software engineering firm.

Industrious and determined, her father started his career consulting, using a small room in the family's modest house in Edmonds as his base of operations. He began by developing software with specific applications for large corporations. Within a short time, he had an enviable reputation for designing software that not only met, but exceeded, his clients' needs. As his reputation grew, so did his list of clients.

Soon after, her father and a select staff of computer programmers, and technical writers and editors were expanding their marketplace and pioneering new areas of software development. Syntronics became synonymous with innovative and quality software. And just four years after her father had established Syntronics, he had amassed a fortune.

Her father had welcomed her into the firm when she was eighteen. When school was in session, she worked part-time. At the start of summer, though, she kept the same hours as the regular employees. She remembered how surprised she was to find herself placed in a junior proofreader's position when first permitted to work at Syntronics, but each year her responsibilities were expanded.

Armed with a Bachelor of Arts degree—a major in English and a minor in Computer Technology—Sam had expected to catapult to the top of her father's company. Instead, she was given an associate editor position reviewing instructional material for the software packages. Eventually, Sam rose to the position of director of communications. It was a position earned from hard work and dedication and not because she was the boss's daughter. Though her father never concealed his pride or his affection, he also never showed favoritism.

Six months earlier, her parents had been killed in a freak accident on the Evergreen Point floating bridge, one of the two bridges that spanned Lake Washington and connected the city of Seattle to the west and the cities of Bellevue and Kirkland to the east. Her parents had been travelling westbound, en route to an evening performance of the Seattle Symphony Orchestra. The police had speculated that because of heavy fog, her father too late saw the stalled vehicle in his lane. He had probably tried to veer right to avoid the stalled truck, one uniformed officer had said, and had been struck from behind by a speeding car. Six people had died that night.

Following the funeral her paternal grandfather, Charles, attempted to fill the void left by her father. Rather than direct Syntronics, he tried to oversee the projects in place. Sam had never been involved in day-to-day operations, so she could offer little real assistance. She believed her father had intended to expose her to the actual management of Syntronics, because a month before his death he had urged her to enroll in basic business administration courses at the university.

She wished now, more than ever, that she had chosen business courses as electives instead of art appreciation, pottery, and the like. Maybe if she had, there would be no need for Jake Sloan.

Before the afternoon had ended, Sam had dialed the telephone number for her grandfather four more times. At six o'clock, she quit trying and went home.

CHAPTER 4

Traffic was so thick on the freeway that Samantha wondered if she would ever reach home. She drove nearly three miles in second gear before the clog of vehicles thinned out enough so that she could drive the speed limit. Not until she took the Redmond exit did she remember that Jill Simms was to visit that night. She pressed the gas pedal harder.

Since Jill had married John Simms two years before, she and Sam had fallen into the routine of meeting several times a month. Sometimes they went shopping, went to a movie, or did nothing more than sit and talk for hours. Since her parent's death, Sam and Jill had only managed two evenings together.

Usually Sam looked forward to these evenings, but not tonight. The scene with Jake had been draining and more than a little depressing and she wished she had remembered earlier that Jill was coming over because she would have postponed their get together. She wasn't going to be good company. She simply couldn't get Jake Sloan out of her mind. Every time she remembered that he had sixty percent of Syntronics and every time she recalled how he had spoken to her, her blood pressure shot up.

Jill's black Honda Civic was parked on the street in the front of the townhouse-style duplex when Samantha maneuvered her used Lexus into the driveway. Jill called a cheery hello from the street as Samantha stepped out of the car. She returned the greeting with a wave and beckoned Jill to walk faster. The temperature had dropped in the last hour and Samantha was anxious to be inside.

Unlocking the front door to her side of the duplex, Samantha apologized for being late. She flipped on a light switch in the entry alcove and moved aside to let Jill enter.

"Make yourself comfortable," Samantha called as she swept past Jill and circled the lower floor turning on lights.

Jill removed her coat and curled up on the loveseat in front of the fireplace. Samantha slipped out of her coat and flung it across the back of a dining room chair. Then she kicked off her high-heel shoes and collapsed into a chair opposite Jill.

"Tough day?" asked Jill.

Samantha nodded, running her hand through her hair. Resting her head against the back of the chair, she closed her eyes, sighed, and then exclaimed, "I never want another Monday like this as long as I live!"

"Let's hope you don't," Jill commented in her most condescending tone. "You look ghastly." Jill, of course, looked as though she had stepped out of the page of a glossy fashion magazine. Even in sweater and slacks, Jill managed to look elegant.

Wanting to see the expression on Jill's face, Sam raised her head. It was clear it wasn't a bit of Jill's dry humor, the tall brunette was serious. Her friend of many years could be brutally honest on occasion, as Sam and others had learned. The two girls had been sorority sisters at the University of Washington. At first, Sam had found Jill difficult to get to know, but eventually she had and what Sam expected to be a lifetime friendship had evolved.

A glance at the nearest mirror verified the accuracy of what she knew Jill would call an "astute observation." She really didn't look like herself in the least, the oval-shaped face looked drawn and very pale; there was no longer any blush accenting her high cheek bones, showing off her creamy complexion. Her shapely lips, usually full and a natural deep rose requiring only a tinted gloss, appeared thin and colorless. Her warm hazel eyes, fringed with long dark lashes and below finely arched brows, were too bright and had a glassy sheen. She had to admit she looked terrible. All but her eye shadow had worn off and even it looked blotchy.

She gazed at her outfit, a two-piece coffee-colored silk dress, and was dismayed to find it thoroughly wrinkled. She found it hard to believe she had gone through an entire day looking as she did. No wonder people had stared at her when she left the office.

"You should have said haggard," Samantha told Jill as she padded barefoot into the kitchen, returning several minutes later with a small bottle of white wine and two long-stemmed crystal glasses.

Jill accepted the wine with a smile, picking up where the conversation had left off. "Ghastly. Haggard. Let's not quibble over an adjective. Or is it an adverb. No matter. Just tell mother Jill the nature of your complaint."

Samantha spent the next forty-five minutes recounting the events of the day. Through Sam's tirade, Jill sat patiently sipping wine, watching her friend pace up and down and gesturing frantically. Finally, Sam sat down and Jill asked unemotionally, "Anything else?"

Nearly choking on her wine, Samantha put a cupped hand to her mouth. "Wasn't that enough?"

Carefully setting the wine glass on the closest end table, Jill cast an unapologetic look at Samantha.

"To tell you the truth, Sam, your description of the day wasn't totally coherent." Seeing Sam's face register something akin to amazement, Jill explained, "The emotion came through quite graphically, what with the flailing arms, clenched fists, the grinding teeth, the spittle on your chin..."

"The murderous look in my eyes," finished Samantha with a snap.

Quickly Jill said, "No. But, honestly, I've never seen you so...so..."

"So what?" Samantha watched Jill grope for the right word.

"Frenzied," offered Jill in desperation.

As an explanation, Samantha said, "Jake Sloan has that effect on me."

Jill replied that she understood the extreme stress Sam was under. The extension of sympathy made Samantha feel ashamed for her curtness.

"Oh Jill. I'm sorry. The situation is so distressing and that...that man is so infuriating."

"Forget Jake Sloan" Jill said casually. "Ignore him, or better yet, wish him away."

Samantha didn't think she would ever be able to forget him, and she certainly couldn't ignore him because it was fairly obvious from today's meeting with him that he wasn't going to permit her to ignore him. Jake most definitely had a way of making his presence known, regardless of where he was.

And wishing him away wouldn't work. No, for the present, at least until she spoke with her grandfather, she had to dance to his tune. She told Jill as much.

"Simply pretend to dance to his tune as you so elegantly put it." There was also a mischievous side to Jill. "Drag those thespian skills of yours out of moth balls." At the university, Sam and Jill had been active members of the drama club.

Samantha laughed. "And you have the audacity to sneer at my turn of phrase!"

"Seriously," Jill reached for the bottle of wine to replenish her now empty glass, "throw darling Jake a few curves."

Taking the remark literally, Samantha said spiritedly, "Are you out of your mind? Flirting with Jake would be suicidal. The man is not a eunuch!"

"I hope not. It would be a terrible waste. The man is beautiful—you heard me—beautiful and sexy. A definite ooh la la."

The remark was made carelessly and was, Samantha knew, without substance. Jill was deeply in love with her husband, John. The attraction between the two was baffling. Jill, statuesque, striking, and always impeccably dressed, had a sharp mind, sharp wit, and a blunt manner. John had an equally sharp brain, but there the similarities ended. Two inches shorter than his wife, John was merely pleasant looking.

He dressed carelessly and spoke his mind only when pressed to do so.

Curiosity had once prompted Samantha to ask Jill why she had chosen John as a mate. Jill's answer had been flabbergasting. "I'm the fulfillment of John's wildest fantasy. Why should he ever look at another woman when he has me? Devotion, admiration, and fidelity are assured with John. Besides, I always liked teddy bears." Jill was nothing if not logical and rational.

Samantha didn't have to think twice about discarding Jill's suggestion as ridiculous.

"I'll wait for my grandfather to get my answers," Sam said determinedly.

"How long are you going to wait?"

"As long as I have to. What choice do I have?"

"There's Jake."

"Never." Samantha slapped the arms of the chair to emphasize her determination to wait.

"Okay, Sam, but if you want your answers and your grandfather is unavailable, what other choice do you have?"

"There has to be another way," Samantha was adamant. Nothing could persuade her to throw herself into Jake's arms. She wouldn't make that mistake again. She emptied her wine glass.

Jill tilted her head to one side, put a finger to her lips, and said, "Ah ha." She looked pleased with herself, but then Jill frequently looked pleased with herself.

"Ah ha, what?" demanded Sam, her curiosity piqued.

"You find him attractive." It wasn't a question.

"Certainly not," said Samantha indignantly, though the flush to her face told Jill otherwise.

Jill was unconvinced. "Sam, I told you that I think the man is an absolute prime example of masculinity. Now don't tell me that you don't find him attractive!"

"I don't find him attractive."

"Why don't I believe you?"

"I don't know," Sam said matter-of-factly. "Why don't you believe me?"

Sam reached for the bottle of wine. Finding it empty, she went to the kitchen to get another, leaving Jill to her own thoughts.

Samantha returned to the living room carrying a bottle in one hand, and a small plate of cheese, crackers, and sliced apples in the other.

"So, tell me. Why don't you believe me?" She allowed Jill to take an apple slice before choosing a small slice of cheese on a cracker for herself.

Between bites, Jill speculated openly. "There's a certain, umm, look in your eyes every time you say his name."

"It's not passion," Sam interjected lightly. "It's murder, remember?"

"I don't think it's the latter. Oh, yes, you're furious, and rightfully so. You're in an intolerable situation. And I really do sympathize. Gospel. But there's more behind your anger with Jake than his sudden appearance at Syntronics. You know him, don't you? From some earlier time in your life, I mean."

Samantha poured herself another glass of wine and grabbed an apple slice for herself. Not until she had taken two bites did she respond to Jill's question.

"The Sloans and the Wards were neighbors for several years. In fact, we were all friends, though most of the socializing was between my parents and Jake's parents. To Jake, I was just a schoolgirl. He was in college and had his own circle of friends so there were few, very few, times when we both were included in any social activities between the two families. Unfortunately, the friendship ended tragically when I was eighteen." She set her plate aside, saying, "Actually, I'm surprised you don't remember the incident. It made headlines."

"I'm a transplant from Oregon, remember?"

"The incident rated copy in the newspapers there, too. In fact, it went national."

Sam continued her story. "Dad and Tyler Sloan shared a common obsession—sailing. Whenever they were together it was impossible to change the subject to any other topic. They would argue for hours over the most trivial aspects of sailing. One day the disagreement would be about who the best builder was or what brand of sailcloth was best. The next day, the argument would be over design features—pros and cons. But there were occasions when they found some small point of agreement. Well," she paused and replenished her glass, "the arguing stopped long enough for them to plan a two-week trip sailing to Canada. The trip excited them. They spent hours bent over navigational charts, sharing a bottle of scotch, and exchanging stories about their individual sea adventures. They sailed on a Saturday. Two days later Jake's father was dead and mine lay in the intensive care unit of Virginia Mason in critical condition. Days passed before Dad could tell us what happened."

"Dad and Mr. Sloan opened up a bottle of scotch an hour after leaving Seattle. There had been weather reports of gale warnings the night before their departure. The sky was a brilliant blue the morning they were sailing so they ignored the reports. They were anxious to start the trip you see. Mr. Sloan was a politician and often didn't have more than a few days of relaxation. And, Dad, well he was a workaholic. So both my mother and Mrs. Sloan were in favor of the trip."

Sam paused, taking a deep breath before she continued. "As I said, Dad and Mr. Sloan opened a bottle of scotch for a toast. It was sort of an inauguration ceremony. One toast followed another. When the first bottle of scotch was empty, Mr. Sloan opened another. Dad quit drinking but Mr. Sloan didn't. Five hours out the weather changed. Dad became anxious and urged Mr. Sloan, who was playing helmsman, to head for the nearest safe harbor. I suppose by then Mr. Sloan was quite drunk. He refused to yield to Dad's request, saying that it was probably just a little storm. They were approaching Deception Pass—known to all sailors for its treacherous waters—when the gale hit. Mr. Sloan couldn't control the tiller. Dad had tried the engine, but it wouldn't turn over. They were listing perilously close to the shoals. Dad was frantic. Mr. Sloan simply couldn't be reasoned with."

"In desperation, Dad lunged at Mr. Sloan, hoping to wrench the tiller away. Mr. Sloan struggled with Dad and Dad ended up clutching the deck for his very life. He was in that position when the boat was smashed against the shoals; his left leg was crushed. When Dad looked back, Mr. Sloan was no longer at the helm. The next time the boat struck the shoals, Dad was thrown overboard onto the rocks. God knows how, but he managed to make it back to the shore. Hikers found him there the next morning."

Fatigue had begun to weaken her voice. She ended the story with, "That's it." It wasn't the end of the story, but she didn't want to share anything else with Jill. Some things needed to remain secret, even from intimate friends.

Samantha had expected Jill to say something, but what she said was unexpected.

"Why," mused Jill, "would an avid and experienced yachtsman consume so much alcohol that he would be unable—unfit—to keep his wits about him? It's rather a contradiction, isn't it? To be a dedicated seafaring man means safety first and foremost. Drinking is something an amateur might do."

At the time of the incident, Jake had said much the same thing. Only his questions and denials had been expressed with extreme anger. Curiously, the newspapers had raised the same questions. Samantha was sure that Jake had inspired, if not supplied, the copy for those questions.

"I don't know why Mr. Sloan drank," Samantha said with honesty.

"And now Jake is at Syntronics."

"With sixty percent interest," added Samantha wearily. "Controlling interest."

"Better try your grandfather again. Maybe he's returned from his trip. The sooner the mystery is solved the better." Jill lowered her legs and slipped on her shoes.

"Leaving?"

"Yes. It's ten o'clock. John expected me an hour ago. Besides, you need your beauty rest."

Samantha started to rise from her chair only to have Jill tell her to remain seated, she would show herself out.

"No," Samantha stood. "I need to lock the door behind you."

"Okay," Jill said, heading for the front door. She opened it and turned back to Sam saying, "Don't worry, everything will work out." She hugged Sam, who managed to smile slightly, and then was gone.

Another hour passed before Samantha could crawl between cool sheets. Though physically exhausted, sleep eluded her. On impulse, she tried her grandfather's phone again. Still no response. Sometime just before three in the morning, she drifted into a fitful slumber.

Chapter 5

Samantha woke late the next morning with a horrendous headache. Not even three tablets of a potent painkiller hastily swallowed could check the pounding in her head. Dark circles under her eyes, telltale signs of a nearly sleepless night, were camouflaged with a skillful application of makeup.

In preparation for the ten a.m. meeting with Jake, she had dressed with more care than usual. Slender and just over five-foot-six-inches in stocking feet, Sam was able to wear any style of clothing, but preferred those that set off her figure and her coloring. Today she had rummaged through her closet and had selected a very tailored navy suit with matching shoes. After adding jewelry to complement the ensemble she wore, she looked in the mirror, pleased to see a reflection of the image she wanted—the picture of a well-dressed, sophisticated woman with an air of independence. Only furrowed brows marred the picture, another result of her throbbing head, which she was sure was the beginning on one of her sinus headaches. In every other respect, her armor was complete, including the defiance in her eyes.

The clock on her car's dashboard showed 9:20 a.m. when she turned the car off 405 onto the Bellevue exit. There were four traffic signals between the exit and Syntronics. Each one was red. Samantha swore softly as she parked the car in the underground garage. The last thing she wanted was to be late, but she was, by a full ten minutes. It took her that long to race into the building, retrieve the SALCOMP file, and reach the workstation outside her father's former office.

Carol, who had been with Syntronics for eight years, greeted Samantha with a warm smile and a hearty good-morning. Samantha squeezed out a hello between counts of ten as she fought to regain a more relaxed composure. Finally Carol nodded her approval and gave Samantha two thumbs up.

Obstinacy propelled Samantha into Jake's office. She had taken no more than five steps when the smile she had forced to her lips turned to a frown. Seeing Jake comfortably seated behind the executive desk from which her father had directed the company set her blood racing, her heart pounding. She didn't acknowledge Jake's charge of being late. She was too busy scanning the office, looking for other familiar objects; there were none. Unbelievably, Jake had redecorated the office. Gone were the wing-backed leather chairs and matching couch, the mahogany bookcase, the paintings depicting sailboats and clipper ships, and the many other personal items, treasured by her father, which had added to the casual comfort Anthony Ward had preferred when conducting business. Now there were chairs of shining chrome and bright fabric, an assortment of green plants, and large abstracts with colors complementing the office furnishings. The room gave one the impression of light and space. It was an impersonal room, revealing nothing about its occupant. She resented the changes as much as the man who made them. Samantha glared at Jake.

"If you're quite finished glaring at the furniture...and at me," drawled Jake, "let's get down to business." He directed Samantha to a seat with a slight movement of his right hand.

Samantha sat, her back ramrod straight, her eyes blazing. Being in Jake's presence, having to witness him settle into a routine at Syntronics, was intolerable. Never before had she reacted so violently to a situation, but then the situation was unique. Until she communicated with her grandfather, Jake had command of her life for eight hours a day. He could tell her when to sit, when to stand, what to do and how to do it. Not even her father, as her employer, had wielded that much power over her. She hated the power Jake had, hated the situation, and hated herself for being too weak to tell him to go to hell and suffer the consequences.

Jake held a pen between thumb and forefinger of his left hand, rolling it back and forth. "Tell me about the SLACOMP project."

"John Simms could explain it better than me," she replied. According to Carol, Jake had already met with department heads, so he surely must know about the SALCOMP project.

"I'm not asking John, I'm asking you." He placed the pen on the desk, his attention on her.

"What do you want to know?" She adjusted the files on her lap.

"Everything. I know nothing." Well-manicured hands were extended palms up as if to show they were empty. Samantha wasn't foolish enough to believe his statement.

"All right," she began "I'll do my best. SALCOMP. It's an acronym for Syntronics Alternative Computer Programs. The project is the most ambitious we've ever undertaken, primarily because we've defined a broader market. We're targeting small businesses, and the home user."

"Through extensive research, using questionnaires, conducting interviews, telephone surveys, et cetera, we were able to identify what software applications were most desirable." Caught up in the excitement of describing the project, Samantha momentarily forgot her hostility toward Jake and spoke more easily.

"A user-friendly word-processing program, a simple spreadsheet, a mail program, and an easy record management package topped the list. To get quality programs, consumers must buy each program separately and pay hundreds of dollars for each. We've assembled all four programs into one low-cost, integrated package."

"Our programs are an improvement over others currently available. We've taken the best and made it better. Simplifying, enhancing, deleting, and adding where necessary. This time," she said with conviction, "Syntronics will be the leader instead of the follower."

Jake was smiling. "So your work stimulates you." She hadn't said so, but it was true nevertheless. Her work meant everything to her. She was a career woman and had decided long ago that marriage and children were unnecessary encumbrances. She wondered what Jake's reasons were for never marrying.

Before she could think of any reasons, Jake spoke to her. "How many brands of computers have programs been written for?"

"Six," thinking hard. "No, seven."

"And instructional materials have been adapted for each?"

"Yes."

"Is the instructional material ready for production?"

"Nearly," she said vaguely.

Jake snatched at the remark with alarming alacrity. "What do you mean, nearly?"

Samantha was saved from having to explain by the phone ringing.

Jake, his eyes riveted on her, picked up the handset.

"Yes, Carol, what is it?" He listened and then said, "Okay, put him through."

"Hello. Yes. Just a minute," he moved the phone away from his ear and covered the receiver with a hand. "Excuse me, Sam. This is a private call."

Samantha needed no other cue to leave. She clutched the files tightly as she made her escape. Jake told her to close the door. It was nearly closed when she heard him say, "Okay Charles. She's gone. Now tell me why the hell you haven't told her the truth." Sam wanted to rush back into the room, to insist Jake let her speak with her grandfather. Instead she found herself committing the same crime she had accused Jake of the day before. She eavesdropped.

Samantha spent a solitary lunch hour trying to make sense of the conversation she had overheard between Jake and her grandfather. The conversation had removed her last vestiges of doubt. There was a conspiracy! Her grandfather calling Jake, and not her confirmed it.

Little had been said by Jake to reveal the reason for the conspiracy. Jake had uttered yes several times, and she heard him say no at least twice. She even heard him say, "Tell her the truth." But what was the truth?

Absorbed with the question, Samantha didn't hear John enter her office. He cleared his throat with a loud harrumph to make his presence known. It still startled her.

"Good heavens, John," She said accusingly. "You scared me out of a year's growth."

Seeing Sam's pensive face, John made a great show of assuming a military stance, raising his hands in surrender, and yelling, "I didn't do it!"

Unamused, Samantha shot John a withering look. "Stow the jokes, John, and you can come in."

John pulled out a chair and sat down, saying, "I'm sorry, Sam."

Thinking she was referring to scaring the wits out of her, Sam said, "You really didn't scare me that badly, John."

"That wasn't why I said I was sorry. Not that I'm not for having scared you." The words were said clumsily, but were meant sincerely.

"What are you sorry about then?"

"About the turn of events," said John.

"Oh, yes," catching his meaning. "The turn of events." Her eyebrows rose. "What you mean is the arrival of Jake Sloan."

"Indirectly."

Pressing her hands to her eyes, Samantha repeated what she had told John's wife Jill. Only now there was more bitterness in her voice. "My life has been a nightmare since he came." Was it really only two days!

"Sam, don't you think you're being a trifle dramatic?" He sounded like Jill.

"And you've been talking to your wife. Some confidante Jill is!" She wondered how much of last evening's conversation had been shared with John.

"Jill is just concerned," John said in her defense. "So am I, Sam. You're expending a lot of energy battling Jake. He's not a bad man."

"Pardon me if I disagree."

"Sam, you're not giving the man a chance. You had him tried, convicted, and executed before you even met him."

So Jill had kept the secret after all.

"I had good reason."

"Good reason?" John's bushy eyebrows were knotted in a frown. "What good reason?"

She couldn't very well tell John the whole truth, so she abbreviated her reason into one concise sentence.

"His taking over Syntronics is the only reason I need."

"Is it? Right now you're so full of self-righteous indignation that you don't want to see the truth."

Truth, John said. It was almost funny.

"Thanks for the analysis," Samantha said with disgust. "You're a real friend."

John's face fell. "It's because I am a friend that I'm talking to you about this."

"Defending Jake Sloan you mean," unmoved by the hurt registered on John's face.

"I like him."

"Traitor."

"And you would, too, if you'd give him—and you—a chance."

"Never."

"Okay, Sam," he shook his head in resignation, "but I have a feeling you'll be sporting some ugly bruises before this is over."

Samantha didn't try to stop John's departure. Her head was throbbing violently; the pressure behind her eyes was unbearable. The pain was so intense she was beginning to have difficulty focusing. From experience she knew what was ahead.

She struggled to her feet and walked as quickly as she was able to the women's restroom just down the hall. Leaning against a sink, she laid a cool towel against her forehead and eyes. The relief the remedy offered was minimal.

It was sheer bad luck that the moment Sam decided to return to her office for medication Jake would be in the corridor. He called her name and she twisted around awkwardly.

"What's wrong?" He demanded, blocking her path.

"Nothing," she said flatly, trying to maneuver around him. He stopped her progress by grasping her upper arm. When she tried to pull free his hold tightened.

"What's wrong?" he repeated.

Samantha's bottom lip quivered, and she hated herself for showing weakness. "I have a…headache."

"A headache?" There was no compassion in his voice.

"Yes, a headache, a sinus headache. I need my purse," she said with effort.

Standing at right angles to each other, Jake and Samantha were making passage through the corridor difficult, not to mention attracting the interest of a several people. Annoyed, Jake relaxed his hold on Samantha, escorted her into her office, and guided her into a chair.

"Where's your purse?" Jake asked, frowning down at her. Wiping away a tear, Samantha pointed to the general vicinity where she had placed her purse. Jake handed her the black leather bag seconds later. She fumbled with the clasp until he relieved her of the task. A single push with his thumb and the clasp released.

"What am I looking for?" He was holding the purse as if he was something distasteful.

"Pill box."

He started pulling things out of her purse. "How on earth do you fit everything in this small space," he began. "There's makeup, brush, keys. No pillbox."

"I must have left it in my other purse." She massaged her temples. Keeping her eyes closed minimized the pain.

"Then it's home for you."

Samantha, having reached the decision before him, rose unsteadily. She removed her still open purse from Jake's possession and extracted her car keys with a shaky hand.

"You're not driving yourself home." He declared seeing her intent.

"Yes, I am," she retorted stubbornly.

Before she could move, Jake plucked the car keys out of her hand saying emphatically, "You're not driving."

Extending her arm toward him with an open hand, she said wearily, "Give me my keys." She wasn't in the mood to argue with him.

"No," he said sternly, shoving the keys in his pocket.

"Please give me the keys." A sharp pain shot across her eyes. She pressed a hand to her brow.

"I never say no twice." He said quietly, but Samantha shrank from him. Her arm dropped. She was too tired to fight with him.

Opening the only closet in her office and finding it empty, he asked, "Where's your coat?"

"I...didn't...wear a coat," she stuttered. She just wanted to pain to stop.

"You didn't wear a coat? In this weather?" The closet door was closed with a loud bang, making her jump. "You little fool, no wonder you're ill."

As casually as if it were his right, Jake walked over to her and draped an arm around her shoulders. Her body stiffened with the contact. Breathing shallowly, Sam tried to wriggle free. The more she wriggled, the more pressure Jake exerted to secure his hold. A harshly whispered, "Stop it," from Jake arrested her struggling as he led her out of the office to the receptionist area. He paused at Karen's desk long enough to remove Samantha's car key from its ring and to hand it over to the startled girl with instructions to have someone bring Samantha's car around.

Jake moved Sam to the elevators and past the bold stares of three of her subordinates. The expression on their faces told Samantha that within a few hours Jake's arm resting across her back would escalate into something much more sordid. She moaned at the thought that her name would soon be romantically linked with Jake. She was relieved when the elevator doors closed behind them.

Jake maintained his proprietary hold on her until they reached the car. When he closed the door behind her, Samantha slipped as close to the door as she could. She hadn't been surprised to know that Jake drove a stylish black Porsche Boxster.

"Nice ride," she muttered absently as he navigated his way into moving traffic.

"Thanks," said Jake, braking at a stoplight.

"Left here," directed Samantha.

He turned his head right and looked at her profile. "I know where you live."

She shouldn't have been surprised, but she was. Without looking at him, she stated, "Is there anything you don't know about me?"

Jake glanced at her between lane changes. "Very little." He accelerated to merge into freeway traffic.

Unable to think of an answer, she laid her head against the leather seat and peered out of the window. With the windows tightly shut, she couldn't hear the rain that now was falling steadily. She heard only the soft whir of the windshield wipers as they swished back and forth.

The distance between Syntronics and her house was long, but it was short enough to make conversation unnecessary. One minute they were on the freeway and the next minute Jake was unlocking her front door. She left him standing in the living room while she went in search of her medication.

When she re-entered the living room, Jake was crouched in front of the fireplace, crumpling newspaper and stuffing it underneath logs. He struck a match and ignited the paper. The seasoned logs stacked on the andirons caught fire. Drawing the wire gate closed, he backed away, brushed off his hands and sat down where Jill had the night before.

Samantha experienced a twinge of annoyance at the ease at which Jake had made himself at home. He had discarded his suit jacket and loosened his tie. From all appearances, he was very comfortable, but then most people were in her home.

Artfully arranged furnishings added to the cozy comfort of the ground floor living area. Gaily patterned and solid print pillows in shades of blue were tossed upon a loveseat and two overstuffed chairs covered in a cream twill fabric. A handmade afghan spilled out of a wicker basket near a potted fern. Above the fireplace hung a watercolor depicting the Seattle waterfront. On the mantle, an antique clock, a gift from her parents, was flanked by silver candlesticks that had once belonged to her grandparents. Scattered throughout the room were African violets in natural clay pots and needlepoint boxes in varying sizes and shapes.

She wasn't aware that he knew of her presence until he said "Why don't you sit down in here, I built the fire because it seemed a bit chilly."

It was irksome to be invited to sit in one's own home. Pushing back an ugly retort, Samantha sat. Jake leaned forward, resting his elbows on his knees.

"Feeling better?" Was it concern she heard?

"Yes." It was true, the pain was not so intense.

"How often do you get these headaches?"

"A few times a year. They're usually most intense in autumn, when it's starting to get damp again."

"I never knew a sinus headache could be so debilitating."

"Obviously you have good sinuses."

"I suppose I have." He sat back, crossed his legs, and continued to stare at her. "Sleepy?"

"Yes," She confessed. "A side effect of the medication. I'd rather be asleep without pain, than be awake with it." The medicine was strong and usually took effect immediately. She was having trouble keeping her eyes open.

Her cell phone rang and Sam started to get up and retrieve it from her purse, but Jake motioned her to remain seated. She couldn't believe that he had the gall to answer her phone. She could tell from his relaxed manner that he knew the caller. He confirmed her impression by handing her the telephone and saying that it was her grandfather.

Grabbing the phone, Samantha said, "Granddad, where are you?" There was so much static on the line, she couldn't hear him. She repeated the question and heard him answer. She wanted to ask him why he had been communicating with Jake and not her, but she didn't dare. Jake would know she had eavesdropped.

"What did you say?" The connection was very poor. Her grandfather was two thousand miles south of Seattle in Baja, California, visiting old friends.

He yelled that he wanted her to join him for dinner on Saturday. She shouted back that she looked forward to it and asked what time. Seven o'clock was the last thing she heard before the phone went dead.

"I guess there was a storm or interference or something," her voice drifted off as she smothered a yawn. "Anyway, it was a bad connection." She was thinking how far away Saturday was. Four days. Four days before she could get any answers.

"So he said." Jake, too, seemed to be adrift in his own thoughts.

If Jake was wondering why Samantha made no comment about his brief exchange with her grandfather, he certainly wasn't telling. From that conversation alone it would have been obvious to anyone that they weren't strangers.

Sometime during the silent interlude after the call from her grandfather, Samantha dozed off. Hours later she woke to find herself in bed, a comforter tucked about her, and a note from Jake on the pillow. Two words were scribbled across a piece of scrap paper: Sweet dreams. She crumpled up the note into a small ball that fit into the palm of her hand, and pitched it into the trash.

Chapter 6

The next day people viewed Samantha with brazen curiosity. She met each questioning gaze with an extra friendly good morning and a dazzling smile. It was the only way she knew to deal with potential gossip.

The sight of John resting against her desk when she entered her office didn't please her. She wasn't up for a discussion about any subject this morning, particularly if it involved Jake. She really should have remained at home, but she couldn't bear the thought of a day passing at Syntronics with Jake at the helm and her not knowing what was going on. She gave John a compulsory greeting, and then went about her early morning routine as if he wasn't there.

Oblivious to her blatant rudeness, John waited patiently, watching Samantha hang up her coat, put away her purse, and then sit down and power on her computer to check email. Not until she was seated did John twist around to face her.

"You look terrible, Sam."

"Thanks, John." She opened a drawer, pulled out folders, and slammed them on top of her desk.

"Oh-h-h," crooned John, "still in a temper." He slid off the desk.

"I'm just not in the mood for small talk, John." The headache was gone, but the temper wasn't. The morning had brought new questions and new fears about Jake's presence at Syntronics. His presence in her home last night, and the fact that he had carried her to bed, was a great source of annoyance. The less contact she had with Jake, the better she liked it.

"I can see that. I just came in to extend an invitation to dinner on Saturday. Jill's planning a Mexican food feast."

Samantha put on a friendlier face. "Thanks, John. And thank Jill. But I'm having dinner with Granddad on Saturday."

"So at least you'll have some answers."

Rifling through files, she retorted, "I certainly have plenty of questions."

"Don't we all," John remarked. "We're not all in a position to ask questions though. Some of us," he pointed to himself, "are mere peons following orders and collecting a paycheck every two weeks for services rendered."

"John," she felt so weary "you're an invaluable member of Syntronics. Without your expertise in programming there might never have been a SALCOMP project."

The compliment had him grinning from ear to ear. "Thanks, Sam. Speaking of SALCOMP, I was given orders this morning to move full speed ahead." Jake certainly wasn't wasting any time she thought.

"By the way, when was the last time you reviewed the instructional material your staff has been preparing?"

"Oh," Sam replied, mentally counting the time, "about two weeks ago." Since her father's death, she had become a trifle slack in her work. Her usual zest and enthusiasm had definitely waned.

John's eyebrows rose at the information, prompting her to ask why he was inquiring.

"Haven't you reviewed any of the material?"

Defensively, "Of course I have, but not in the last two weeks."

"Jake's had the material since Monday afternoon," John informed her.

"Oh." She shifted uncomfortably in her chair. She certainly hoped her staff had been productive.

"Be prepared," John warned.

Samantha almost laughed. Be prepared, he said.

It was funny. She had never been less prepared for anything in her life.

"John," throwing the ball back in his court, "just how do you suggest I prepare myself? To my knowledge there's no anecdote for the kind of pain Jake Sloan inflicts. And if there were, it would have a short shelf life."

John stepped back and gave her a searching look.

"You really don't like him, do you?" It wasn't a question; it was more a slow recognition and admission to fact. Sam responded anyway.

"I seem to be the only one here who hasn't joined the Jake Sloan fan club," she said rather heatedly. "And you, by your own admittance, are one of his greatest admirers."

John bristled at the unflattering remark. "Yes," he admitted, "I like him. I told you that yesterday and you climbed on your high horse." He saw her reaction to the statement and continued, "Oh yes you did. He's a man of action and, frankly, he's exactly what Syntronics needs."

"Needs?" echoed Sam. "What exactly do you mean?" John seemed reluctant to clarify his statement so she prodded him.

She sat back in her chair, arms folded. "Come on, John. Let's hear it." Best to hear it now, she thought.

John hesitated and Samantha stepped in again, urging him to speak.

"Okay, Sam," he said calmly. "I know from Frank Smith in accounting that the company has been experiencing serious financial difficulties for some time. Even before your father died the company was making only modest profits for years. Syntronics relied heavily—too heavily—on tried and true markets. Everyone else in the industry has been pumping money into research and development, and reaping the monetary rewards for their efforts. Quite frankly, if SALCOMP doesn't hit the market soon, before competitors get the jump on us, Syntronics may cease to exist."

John was only verbalizing what she had suspected. How many times had she pushed her suspicions aside, ignored the obvious, afraid to face the truth. Samantha knew John expected her to say something. Before obliging him, she chose her words carefully.

"I've known for some time about our financial posture. Why do you think I so strongly supported the development of SALCOMP? I'm all too aware that the project must be successful." The number of clients requiring specialized programming had dwindled over the years, and for the small market available, competition had grown fierce. More and more organizations purchased over-the-counter products, which hurt smaller businesses like Syntronics.

"If you know all that, Sam, then you should be grateful that Jake is now in charge."

Samantha gripped the edge of her desk. "Grateful, John? Why should I be grateful?"

The sudden flare of indignation caught John by surprise. He attempted to pacify her by rephrasing his statement.

"Okay, thankful. You should be thankful."

"How about neither," she snapped.

"Sam," he said with a sigh. "Be realistic. Jake can save this company. He may be young, but look what he did with Krage Industries three years ago. They were on the verge of bankruptcy and he turned them around. Hell, they were ranked 250 in Fortune 500 last year. And look how he breathed life into Pacific West. If it hadn't have been for Jake's special skills, his shrewdness, and, yes, his ruthlessness, Pacific West would be a memory and over two thousand people instead of a few hundred would be unemployed."

Sam grudgingly acknowledged the accuracy of John's brief description of Jake's successes. At the time, even she had marveled at Jake's seemingly invincible Midas touch when it came to saving floundering businesses. Is that why her grandfather had brought Jake in, she wondered. Because he believed Syntronics needed Jake's special skills? SALCOMP would fix the problem. It just had to.

John brought her back into the present. "Sam, you better read the instructional material today."

"I will. Thanks, John."

"Sure. What are friends for?"

"For speaking the truth, even when you don't want to hear it."

John recognized the apology and accepted it without comment.

After he left, Samantha decided it was too close in her office. She needed more space in which to think.

Grabbing her purse and her coat, she rushed out of the office. She stopped to tell Karen that she had a business appointment downtown, and that she would return after lunch.

Thirty minutes later she was parking the car across from the pier in downtown Seattle. For the first time in days it wasn't raining. The sky was a brilliant blue, and there were no clouds on the horizon.

She had fabricated her business appointment; the desire to escape had been that strong. It wasn't in her nature to lie, at least not about important things. Climbing the steps to the marketplace, she thought of the lies she had told in the last two days. There weren't many, she decided as she entered the center of the marketplace.

Samantha always found the marketplace a fun place to be. Eventually she strolled into an open area perched high enough to provide a panoramic view of Elliot Bay. A jumbo jet soared overhead, reminding her of a trip the year before.

She had been returning from two beautiful weeks in Mexico. A young girl in the window seat had bombarded Sam with questions upon learning she was a born and bred Washingtonian. Eventually the questions changed from what kind of clothes people wore to what the city of Seattle offered.

Samantha began by describing the Seattle pier and the marketplace, which had been renovated and given new life by a group of Canadian investors. It had been easy to describe the marketplace and its colorful collection of fruit and vegetable stands that shared space with fishmongers and local artisans peddling their wares.

Next she told the girl—she had forgotten her name—about the Seattle Center, once the site of a World's Fair. She did her best to describe the Center's many features, including the food court, the Space Needle with its revolving restaurant, and the monorail that connected the Center to downtown.

There had been times during the conversation when Samantha had felt like a travel log come to life. She had talked about the University District, Green Lake, the Ballard Locks, Pioneer Square, and the International District. She even suggested some Chinese dishes the girl should sample and the restaurants in the International District that offered them. After detailing the locations as best she could, she described special events like Fat Tuesday, Seattle's answer to Mardi Gras, the regatta, and so on and so forth until she was quite exhausted.

The weather had been of particular interest to the youthful stranger. Samantha had assured her that it wasn't entirely as gloomy as some people tended to suggest. One grew accustomed, she had explained, to the rain and fog in winter. And she adored the flowers—cherry blossoms, tulips, daffodils, irises, mums, crocus, and bleeding hearts—that arrived in spring.

The girl's interest was insatiable; Samantha had been quite relieved when a flight attendant had announced they were landing. She hoped the girl found Seattle as beautiful as she did.

From her concrete perch above the piers, Samantha could see the Seattle ferries as they left their portage for Bremerton and more northern points. There were people entering and exiting the aquarium, the headquarters of the Port of Seattle, and Ivar's, a restaurant noted for its seafood.

Realizing that she hadn't eaten anything since breakfast the day before, Samantha decided to eat at Ivar's. The marketplace had filled with people, making passage throughout the length of the building difficult. Descending the stairs to the pier was easier and in no time she was being seated at a window table at Ivar's.

She ordered a bowl of clam chowder but swallowed only a few spoonfuls before asking the waitress to take it away. Instead of eating, she sipped a soft drink, and wished it were Sunday. The strain of the situation was beginning to take its toll. She wasn't sleeping well, wasn't eating well, and wasn't thinking straight.

By the time Samantha paid the cashier, there was a long line of people waiting for seating. Reluctant to return to the office, Samantha walked around for another half an hour before she went back to the car.

Chapter 7

When Sam did return to Syntronics, she took the back stairs to her office to avoid meeting anyone. Finding a note from Jake posted on her door, Samantha's already low spirits plunged lower. He demanded her presence as soon as she returned. There wasn't even a please on the note. Angrily she crushed the note into a small wad, and threw it into the waste basket. Let him wait, she told herself.

She took an almost wicked pleasure in keeping Jake waiting. His chauvinistic and domineering attitude was extremely irritating. For the next hour, she busied herself returning telephone calls and talking with her staff, something she hadn't done in quite a while. At her request, hard copies of the instructional materials were produced for inspection. She was stunned when a mere hundred pages were placed in her hands.

Sitting down on the spot, she began reading. With the turn of each page, anxiety grew. After scanning just fifteen pages, she realized that a total rewrite was required. Besides glaring grammatical errors, the text was poorly written, with no logical progression. An inexperienced college freshman could have written better content.

Just as she was about to relate her findings to the small group of documentation analysts, her telephone rang. She reached over, picked up the handset, and answered, "Samantha Ward." Jake barked out a single word, "Now!" and then slammed down the phone. Stiffly, Sam hung up. Six pairs of eyes watched her face turn a deep red. No one spoke as she snatched up a notebook and pencil, and issued instructions to be ready to work late beginning the next day. Halfway down the hall someone said loudly enough for her to hear, "What's with her?" They didn't hear her answer, "Jake Sloan!"

The nearer she drew to the executive suite, the more rage she felt. She marched into Jake's office without as much as a hello to Carol. Jake was propped up against the front of his desk, his arms and legs crossed. He told her caustically to close the door and sit down. Sam slammed the door so hard the pictures on the wall rattled and he swore.

Samantha sat primly, bracing herself for a verbal assault. He was standing rigidly, arms akimbo, just to her left.

"I left a message on your desk at one p.m. You returned to the office—oh, yes, I saw you sneak up the back stairs—at two p.m.," he spat. "It's now four p.m. Why the hell did I have to track you down?"

"I had calls to return," she answered hotly, still annoyed by his summons.

"They could have waited."

"They could have, but I couldn't. And I wanted to check on the progress made with the instructional material."

He moved over to the window, his back to her. "And?"

"And what?" she asked cautiously, peering at his back and the shoulders that were as wide as any football players. If he had read the instructional material, he had surely come to the same conclusion she had.

Sam settled back in the chair as he came to stand directly in front of her. He was so near she could smell his aftershave and see the dark hairs on his well-manicured hands. They were large hands, with long tapering fingers. Large enough to fit around my neck she thought.

Jake spun around quickly. "Don't you dare bandy words with me," he warned. "When was the last time you examined what your staff was writing?"

Watching Jake was similar to watching a dark storm gather in the distance. John had asked the same question hours before. She answered with some trepidation. "Twenty minutes ago."

He walked over to the desk again and leaned against it, one hand supporting his weight. His eyebrows were raised, his tone was sarcastic. "Twenty minutes ago." Shoving his hands in his pockets, he asked with a sneer, "And what did you find?"

Her hands were clasped tightly together. Stammering she said, "I found…I found…"

"Let me tell you what you found." Reaching behind him, he grabbed a file folder and flung it in her lap. Sam didn't grab the folder fast enough and its contents spilled onto the floor. She glanced down and her breath caught in her throat. It was the instructional material.

She bent to retrieve the material, but Jake clutched her hand firmly. Instantly every muscle in her body was taut.

"Leave it! The janitors will pick it up with the other trash. That's what it is, isn't it? Trash?"

Afraid to speak, she nodded in agreement while trying to pull her hand free. His hold tightened and she heard the pounding of her own heart.

"Four weeks. Do you hear me? Four weeks and I want the instructional material word perfect. No excuses. By Tuesday I want to see some results." He loosened his grip and pushed her hand toward her with more force than was necessary. Sam rubbed her hand; it felt numb. Some sixth sense warned her not to make a vehement protest about the deadline. He looked extremely dangerous with his mouth twisted in a thin and ugly grimace.

"You do realize how important this project is," he stated bluntly, pulling out his chair.

"Yes, I do," she replied haughtily. The blood was beginning to circulate in her hand again.

"So you're aware that Syntronics has some financial problems."

"I'm not stupid," she retorted sharply. "And I'm not blind."

"At least not all of the time," he commented nastily.

"No one," she began insolently, "needs to tell me how much Syntronics needs SALCOMP to be a success. There are people employed here who have given years, not just a few days, of dedicated service. Each has a vested interest in seeing SALCOMP completed, seeing it succeed. Of course, there's always one person who is motivated by financial gain alone."

Jake's tone was icy, his eyes fiery. "For your own sake," he cautioned, "I suggest you trade that sharp tongue for a sharp pencil and get to work."

Sam was glad a desk separated them. Her pulse was too rapid. During the last two days, Jake had intimidated, insulted, and infuriated her as no one before had done. She had witnessed a display of varying degrees of anger in him, without fully comprehending their source. Now she saw smoldering fury and it was not a comforting sight.

Jake leaned back in his chair and looked at her with such intensity that she felt like something examined under a microscope in a medical laboratory. In the enduring silence, she began to grow self-conscious. It was a new feeling and she didn't like it. She couldn't bare his bold examination. Her lips were as dry as her throat. She moistened them with her tongue. It occurred to her that Jake might interpret the action as a nervous reflex, but she decided she didn't care what he thought.

"Can I go now or is there something else?" Samantha asked, sliding out of her chair and straightening her suit jacket. She was resolved to leave regardless of his answer.

He took his time in replying. His answer, "Not yet," was as ominous and as unnerving as his stare.

"Is that yes, I can go, or no, I can't," she inquired as she stepped on the instructional material on the floor.

"It means you can go. For now." She didn't mistake the ambiguity of his statement. She wished she knew the intent behind his words, but she wasn't going to ask him to explain. She wanted out of the office.

"Then I'll return to my work." Even as she closed the door, she knew his cold blue eyes were still watching her.

Chapter 8

The next two days Sam immersed herself in work, tackling the job of rewriting the instructional material for the SALCOMP project with an intensity that tired those working with her. When six p.m. came on Friday, Syntronics emptied except for Sam and her disgruntled staff who worked until ten.

As she turned off the lights in the building and locked the door, Sam smiled to herself, pleased with the progress made on the rewrites. She was even more overjoyed that an entire two days had passed without even a glimpse of Jake Sloan.

Saturday rolled in on a heavy fog. By noon there was visibility, and by two p.m. rain clouds were blackening the sky. Sam's apprehension was high. She had woken early from yet another troubled sleep with a sense of foreboding that lasted through breakfast into lunch. It was still with her as she backed her car out of the garage in early evening.

A short phone call from her grandfather mid-afternoon confirmed dinner at seven. He allowed her no chance to draw him into conversation, ending the call immediately upon hearing her acknowledgement, which only intensified her feelings.

The drive to her grandfather's house took barely twenty minutes, though tonight the journey seemed much longer. Her hand shook slightly as she pushed the doorbell. Seconds later, the huge oak door swung inward and her grandfather was saying hello. As soon as she crossed the threshold, she again experienced the feeling of impending doom. Dismissing the impression as fanciful, Sam stood on her tiptoes to kiss her grandfather hello, receiving a warm hug in return.

"You look well, Granddad," she said, hanging her coat in the hall closet. His appearance, in fact, was alarming. Just over a week had passed since their last meeting and in that short space of time he had visibly deteriorated. He looked ten years beyond his seventy years. His shoulders were more stooped, the hair more white now than grey. Even his walk appeared sluggish, as if he found no more reason in life to hurry to a destination.

Arm in arm, they walked into the dining room. All through dinner her grandfather chatted about every subject but the one in which she was most interested. Neither ate heartily. Sam used her fork to push food around her plate, taking a bite only occasionally. She noticed her grandfather also was picking at his food, which in itself was odd because he normally was not a fussy eater. By the time his housekeeper served dessert, Sam thought she would explode with frustration.

Unable to suppress her anxiety any longer, she asked, "Granddad. What's happened?"

His fork dropped with a clatter. With an audible sigh he said, "You mean, why is Jake Sloan at Syntronics?" She could hear the weariness in his voice.

"Yes."

Laying his napkin on the table and pushing back his chair, he said "Let's go into the study."

He led and Sam followed. The study, with its huge leather chairs, stone fireplace, and decorous accents reminiscent of a room in an English country house she had once visited, offered a warm, intimate atmosphere. From long habit, Sam chose the chair with a view of the window, opposite the brass-studded wingback that was her grandfather's favorite.

While her grandfather mixed drinks, Sam sat quietly, wondering what dreadful reason he would give for Jake's presence at Syntronics. Anyone who knew her grandfather well would instantly suspect he carried an oppressive burden. Gone were the gregariousness and effervescence that made him such a good companion. In their place was a gravelly and a slightly funereal demeanor, causing her to think that whatever secret he carried, it was truly dreadful.

He had taken an unusually long time to mix two simple drinks. Samantha eyed her grandfather as he handed her a tall glass filled with a golden liquid and then folded his body into his chair. Her brow furrowed in concern. As she sat there and sipped her drink, Sam was torn with mixed emotions, wanting to learn the grim details of the secret and have a tangible problem to dissect, and not wanting to know how to protect an already fragile mental state. Her logic won and she addressed her grandfather.

"Granddad, please. Tell me why Jake is at Syntronics." Adding, "Surely the reason isn't that bad."

His gaze intent on the contents of the glass he clutched, he answered solemnly, "It is."

With effort Sam quelled her exasperation. "Tell me. Let's get it over with. It's obvious that whatever knowledge you possess about Jake's presence at Syntronics is tearing you apart. And it's tearing us apart. Believe me, whatever it is, I can take it." And then from a forced smile, "I'm strong. I come from good, strong stock. Remember?"

She was leaning forward in her chair, showing her readiness to accept his answer. There was none. He opened his mouth to speak, but no words came out. Instead, he emptied the contents of the glass in one gulp, and then went to refill it. Sam sat huddled in her chair, a hand pressed to her forehead. Her frustration level was rising with the passing of each silent minute.

The melodic chime of the front door bell momentarily wrestled her attention away from the dilemma at hand. Turning her chair, she asked her grandfather quizzically, "Were you expecting someone?"

He said only, "I'll answer it," and left. A few moments later he returned, a drink in one hand, an envelope in the other, and Jake Sloan at his heels. As always, the mere sight of Jake accelerated her heartbeat.

Standing and facing her grandfather, Samantha demanded with hostility, "Why is he here?"

"Because I asked him to be here." Her grandfather's admission didn't lesson her anxiety. Samantha shot Jake a withering look and received an expressionless stare in return. She sat, chin jutting and attention riveted on some bookcases to the right of her grandfather's chair, while a drink was poured for Jake.

The envelope was still in her grandfather's grasp as he skirted her chair to reach his own. Jake, still silent, positioned himself near the bookcases, and had a clear view of the two other occupants in the room. Sam looked at her grandfather unhappily.

"Sam, you already know that he," inclining his head towards Jake, "has 60 percent of Syntronics. It's time you know why." The words were clipped, as if he found speaking difficult. "This…letter is the only explanation I can give you. Once you read the letter," he paused with a sigh, "you'll understand why Jake has controlling interest and why I…want…no, beg you, to do as Jake requests."

An unsteady hand held out the envelope. Samantha could only stare at it, suddenly afraid. She quit nibbling nervously on a fingernail and took the envelope offered. Turning it over she lifted the flap, ready to extract the contents. Her grandfather's hand suddenly shot out and covered hers. Startled, Sam looked up and saw pain in his eyes. The envelope fell into her lap as she covered his hand with her own.

"What is it?" She whispered.

He said her name and then broke off with a muffled sound. Reluctantly Sam released his hand and resumed the task he had interrupted. Jake and her grandfather watched. The only sound in the room was the crackling of a dying fire.

Sam gasped when she unfolded a letter and recognized her father's handwriting. Immediately, she looked to her grandfather for an explanation, but his head was bent. Even Jake's eyes were downcast.

The sense of impending doom experienced earlier touched her again as she read the first few lines of the letter that had no salutation.

> *"For years I have carried a heavy burden of guilt. I knowingly defamed the name of a good and honest man. I robbed him of life and deprived a woman of a husband and a son of a father. Not a day has passed that I have not been filled with remorse. And yet, I was too weak to admit to a crime that I committed. Tyler Sloan wasn't responsible for the accident that took his life and left me with a bad leg. He wasn't the one drinking that day, I was. Tyler was at the helm all day, full sails up. Muddled as I was with scotch, I didn't even notice the change in weather, but Tyler did. He tried to start the engine and asked for my help when it wouldn't turn over. By this time, there were strong winds—winds approaching gale force. I managed to crawl toward him, my progress impeded by the wind and, yes, my drunkenness. I, too, attempted to start the engine, and failed.*
>
> *Tyler knew the only chance we had was to drop sails and pray we could make it through Deception Pass. He left me at the tiller and tried to lower the main sail alone. The wind was now at full force. Moving was difficult, remaining upright was difficult. The yacht was pitching wildly. Tyler got the main sail down and was reaching for the jib when the boom broke free. It struck him in the middle of his back and*

he fell to the deck and was dragged to the edge. He was screaming for my help, but I couldn't move.

There was a great heave of the boat and Tyler went over. I hung on for longer. Finally I lost my grip and was tossed over the side but hung on only because my foot was caught in some rope. The boat was being pushed toward the shore. As it crashed, I was thrown free and lay on the rocks until found the next morning by hikers. The remainder of the story you know.

Why did I lie? At the time I simply could not face the ruin I knew would follow a confession. How could I tell my loved ones, my business associates, my friends, and my employees that I was so drunk that I cost a man his life. I truly believe I could have saved him had I been sober. I ask my family to do whatever necessary to make restitution to the Sloans. Over the years I have tried to think of some manner in which I could recompense Tyler's wife and son. They have wealth, so money would be inadequate. Perhaps you can succeed where I have failed.

After Tyler's death I tried my best to be a better father, friend, businessman, and civic servant. I tried everything but admitting the truth. Forgive me.

It was signed simply Anthony. She had expected something awful, but a letter from her father confessing to such a heinous act was beyond even her fertile imagination. Very carefully, Sam folded the letter and inserted it back into the envelope. Her first instinct was to question the authenticity of the letter. After all, she thought, Jake could have handed her grandfather a forged document. She was still looking at it when she said in a monotone voice, "I don't believe it."

"Anthony wrote it," responded her grandfather.

"No. I won't believe that," she shook her head and closed her eyes tightly. "Daddy couldn't have written it. He couldn't have been responsible for Mr. Sloan's death."

"Sam, it's true. That letter was in the hands of your father's attorney and was marked for the eldest living member of the Ward family in the event of Anthony's death. Only you, I, and Jake know about the letter. God, don't you think I wish it wasn't true. For the rest of my life, I have to live with the knowledge that my only son committed a terrible crime!" The anguish in his voice brought tears to her eyes.

"Daddy couldn't..." The denial was again interrupted by her grandfather.

"Oh, Sam. Do you think I wanted to believe it? It's harder for you, isn't it? You loved your father so. In some ways, I think you were somewhat blinded by your father's love and generosity. But then, what child wants to admit that their hero has faults. What father wants to admit his son had some fatal flaw? God knows I didn't want to believe it. And I certainly didn't want to tell you about the letter, but what choice did I have? I couldn't turn Syntronics over to Jake and not eventually tell you why."

"And is that all he wants? Just Syntronics?" Sam didn't trust Jake. Part of her didn't even trust her grandfather at the moment.

Her grandfather hung his head. "No, Sam, that isn't all he wants."

She glanced at Jake, her eyes filled with tears. With a trembling voice she asked, "What else do you want?"

"You." His face was a wooden mask, revealing no emotion at all.

"Me?" Not understanding his meaning.

"You," he reiterated without explanation.

Turning to her grandfather, a knot in the pit of her stomach, "What does he mean?"

Her grandfather glanced at Jake. "He means he wants you as his wife."

"His what?" exploded Sam as she shot to her feet, all color drained from her face.

"My wife," confirmed Jake.

"No!" It was unthinkable!

"Either you consent to…" Jake started with a definite snarl.

"Jake, just a minute," interjected her grandfather. "Sam, do you realize that Jake has a perfect right to publish this letter."

"Publish?"

"Yes, Sam, publish. Jake has a right to clear his father's name. The publicity at the time of the accident cast a black shadow over the Sloans, one that Jake has had to live under all these years."

Samantha had a vision of the exposure of her father's guilt in big, bold print. Such news assuredly would get national attention.

"But why me? Why marriage?" She demanded, her face contorted with anger.

"It's the price he's set for restitution," her grandfather told her gravely.

"And you go along with this?"

Charles Ward took a deep breath. "I'll go along with anything that won't bring further shame to the Wards or further misery to the Sloans."

"So I'm his price," Sam commented sullenly to no one in particular.

Jake answered, "If you want my silence, then yes, you're my price."

"And if I say no?"

"Sam…" came her grandfather's plea, interrupted by Jake's first angry retort.

"Then I'll make sure the world knows that it wasn't my father who was guilty, but yours. He was criminally negligent."

His words were as convincing as his black scowl. There was no doubt that Jake would expose her father even in death.

"So I'm to be the sacrificial lamb," she said weakly as she sat back down, "in payment for my father's crime. I wonder if he ever conceived of the price that would be asked."

There was a misty glaze in her grandfather's eyes when he said, "Sam. If there was any other way…but there isn't. He wants you."

"He wants revenge," stated Sam. Both she and her grandfather had been talking as if Jake wasn't present.

Jake jumped into the conversation saying, "And why the hell shouldn't I? The name Tyler Sloan until ten years ago was highly respected. Fellow politicians, businessmen, and governments used to call my father for counsel. Your father's account of the accident destroyed my father's good name. Even now my mother remains cloistered in a house in

California. She withdrew from society completely after the accident. What payment do I ask for her?"

Sam had no answer for Jake.

"Jake," said Charles Ward sadly, "no payment on earth can restore Tyler's good name, give you back a father, your mother a husband. I don't really want my granddaughter, my only surviving relative, to forsake her own life in payment for her father's guilt and, yet, I can think of nothing else that comes close to the biblical doctrine of an eye for an eye."

The accuracy of her grandfather's statement filled her with sorrow and left no question that Jake's demand would have to be fulfilled.

Sam squared her shoulders and expelled a long sigh. Very quietly she said, "All right."

"What did you say?" Jake asked.

"All right, I'll…I'll marry you," she said with resignation and saw her grandfather's muscles relax. "But I want my father's letter."

Charles Ward's eyes flew to Jake for an answer. A look passed between the men and Jake finally told Sam, "Okay. You'll have the letter."

"When?" demanded Sam.

Jake took his time answering. "You can have the letter after we're married. I'll give it to you at the reception. Is that satisfactory?"

"Yes," Sam confirmed dully. "That's satisfactory."

"Well, then," said a very relieved Charles, "I'll leave you two to work out the details. Forgive me, but I'm very tired."

Bending to kiss her goodnight, her grandfather said in a hushed voice only she could hear, "It'll be okay, Sam." Sam doubted that anything in her life would be okay for some time to come.

With her grandfather's departure, Sam felt even more vulnerable. Jake hadn't taken his eyes off her since she had taken the letter from her grandfather's hand. Now he sat in her grandfather's chair, making it impossible for her to avoid making eye contact with him.

Sam found the idea of discussing a wedding ceremony with Jake as distasteful as the idea of marriage itself. She felt numb and incapable of rational thought. "I can't talk about this tonight," she told Jake, nursing a faint belief that he would concur.

"You'll have to."

His answer, harsh and implacable, destroyed her hope that he felt a small modicum of compassion for the shock she had sustained.

"I can't," she argued.

"You will," he exerted.

It was clear that Jake wasn't going to yield.

Reluctantly she gave in. "All right, Jake, what is it you want to discuss?"

"There's nothing to discuss. We'll be married in one week at a church of your choosing."

"One week! That's impossible."

"No, it isn't," Jake informed her with such assurance that she had no doubt that he had anticipated an affirmative answer from her. He had known she would do anything to protect her father's memory, her family name, and Syntronics.

With more spirit than she felt, Sam announced, "I said I'd marry you, but I will not marry you in a church. It would be blasphemous." It was the only condition on which she thought she might win.

Jake considered her rebellious statement in stony silence before conceding. "Okay, Sam, no church. But if you think that the marriage will be less binding because it's performed by a justice of the peace, think again."

Puzzled, Sam asked, "What exactly do you mean?"

"I mean that this marriage isn't temporary, regardless of who performs the ceremony. And it won't be a marriage in name only."

Sam blanched at the last remark. "You can't expect me to…to prostitute myself!" Her heart was beating so hard she put a hand to her breast.

"Call it whatever you like. But the day you say, I do, then you will—whenever and however I want. This marriage will not end at the bedroom door. There will be no annulment, no divorce."

And no escape she thought. Shaking, she cried, "You can't expect me to be a real wife."

"I not only expect, I demand," he shouted so loudly that she expected her grandfather to come running down the stairs. He followed her eye movement.

"Your grandfather isn't going to rescue you, Sam," he said with amusement. "He supports this marriage. It may not be a marriage made in heaven, but it won't be any less a marriage."

Wearily she said, "My grandfather supports you only because he feels responsible for my fa...father's actions. He shouldn't, and neither should I. But I do and because I do, I'm paying the highest price possible. My freedom. Tell me, Jake, do you really want to marry a woman who loathes the sight of you, who cringes the moment you draw close? Who will never willingly accept your touch, your lovemaking? When you marry me, you'll be marrying an empty shell. Whatever you want from me you'll have to take, because I'll never give it to you without a fight."

Jake threw back his head and laughed, then levelled a look on her that made her heart stop beating. "You little fool. Do you really think your opinion matters to me? It doesn't. Go ahead, my sweet, fight. I've always liked women with spirit."

"In the bedroom you mean," she said nastily. "You resent them in the boardroom."

"In your case, Sam, I'll be in control in both areas," he replied coolly, but Sam knew she had aroused his temper because of the pulsating flex of his jaw muscles.

"So you think," she retorted, not heeding the danger signal.

"As I know," he responded gruffly, his anger now thoroughly roused, the eyes narrowed to small slits.

"I'm tired, Jake, and I want to go home." She knew it sounded as if she was asking for his permission to leave, but she didn't care. Hours before she had crossed the invisible demarcation line between caring and not caring.

"Okay, Sam, no more discussion tonight. But on Monday I'll have a list of things for you to do."

"What things?" she frowned, accentuating the last word.

"Things," mimicking her emphasis on the word. "Necessary things like selecting the engagement ring, getting blood tests. Things like choosing a site for the reception and announcing our engagement."

She wanted to scream at him that she didn't want an engagement ring, was repulsed at the idea of telling the world that she would be Mrs. Jake Sloan, and wasn't interested in a reception for a marriage she considered a sham. Exhaustion was the only thing that prevented her from saying these things to Jake. Utterly drained by the trauma of the evening, it was becoming more and more difficult to engage in a verbal sparring match with Jake. She felt disheveled and longed for a hot bath.

"All right, Jake. Monday." She stood, picked up the drink she hadn't touched, and set it on the bar. When she turned back to retrieve her purse and car keys, Jake was standing between the chairs.

"Excuse me, but I need my purse and car keys."

Jake picked up the keys, dangling them before her. "These car keys?"

"Yes," she reached out for them, but Jake drew them back, holding the keys just out of her reach.

Irritated by the childish play, Sam said caustically, "I'm too tired to play games, Jake."

"There's just one more thing." He threw the keys on the chair.

Sam sighed. "What?"

"This." Before she could protest, Jake had drawn her into his arms, crushing her body against his so hard that her breasts hurt.

"And this," he added, forcing her head back and kissing her with an intensity that robbed her of breath. The more Sam fought to free herself from the embrace, the more demanding the kiss became. Jake's lips plied her own roughly as she continued to struggle, while maintaining a detachment that finally caused him to break off and swear.

He relaxed his hold, but she could still feel the pressure of his fingers in the small of her back. Her face averted, Sam listened as Jake said, "There was a time when you longed for my kisses."

"I didn't know then what an awful brute you are," Sam spat.

Laying his hand along the side of her face, Jake applied enough pressure to pull her face in front of his.

"Brute?" Jake whispered, placing a kiss on her forehead. "How unkind you are, sweet Sam. I can be as loving and tender as any man." In demonstration, his index finger traced the outline of her brow, stroked her cheek, and softly brushed across her lips.

"Of course," he kissed the hollow space under her chin, "I like being met half way." Sam remained perfectly still, bent on remaining cold and unreceptive to his advances. Jake cupped her face and began kissing her again. This time his lips were soft and warm; the kiss gently beckoning her to respond. When he at last elicited a soft cry from her, the kiss became more urgent, the embrace tighter as he tried to mold his body to hers. Frightened by the sensations his lovemaking was generating, Sam started struggling again, beating on his chest.

He pushed her away and held her at arm's length, a satisfied smile on his face. Sam was breathing heavily, her chest heaving, her face flushed from the struggle. She couldn't look at him, too embarrassed at having responded to his caresses. He looked at her curiously, as if he had just learned something new about her.

His voice was low, his eyes bright, "Run, Sam, or I won't wait till our wedding night."

And she did.

Chapter 9

Samantha had run so hard and so fast that it wasn't until she was luxuriating in a hot bath, reliving the harrowing events of the evening, that she realized she had left her purse and cell phone at her grandfather's. It had been nearly midnight when she collapsed in her living room, crying steadily for an hour.

She wept for her father and all the lonely moments he must have known the last years of his life, harboring a painful secret, a guilt he could share with no one. She wept for her grandfather, for Jake's parents, and even for Jake himself. Last of all, she wept for herself and the bleak future ahead of her as Mrs. Jake Sloan. When she could cry no more, she went upstairs and prepared a bath.

The bath soothed the tension of her body, but nothing could eradicate the thoughts that tormented her. One minute she was admonishing herself for giving in with barely more than a whimper to Jake's blackmail and the next minute feeling cowardly and plotting an escape from Seattle before there could be a wedding. Then she would think of her father, the reputation he had held in the business community; the charitable acts he had performed; his commitment to live honorably; to treat all persons fairly and equally; and to strive for excellence in every endeavor. The letter would then intrude on her thoughts and she found herself reviewing her father's life, questioning everything he had ever said, anything he had ever done.

The memory of Jake's kisses and her momentary surrender inflicted its own special agony and evoked an older memory, one she had buried deep. Jake had spoken truthfully when he said there had been a time when she longed for his kisses. But she had been an adolescent then, given to romantic fantasy, yearning for womanhood without fully comprehending what it meant.

She had started dating at 16—not high school seniors, but college freshmen. By the time she was seventeen, she was involved with an older crowd. There were parties off campus in the frat houses and in private residencies. Occasionally, she would catch a glimpse of Jake at the parties. Sometimes he was alone and sometimes he wasn't. Never did she see him with the same date twice.

On the first occasion when Jake saw her at a party, his face registered surprise. At parties thereafter, each time Jake saw her he went out of his way to say hello. Not once did he make an outright suggestion that the people and the format of the parties were beyond her years, despite her attempts to dress and to act more sophisticated than she actually was. He did, however, ask if her parents were aware of her weekend activities. Her reply had been flippant, and Jake had made reference to children playing at being adults, drawing laughter from all those within earshot. His remark had stung and a humiliated Sam had insisted her escort take her home.

One Saturday, almost one month past her seventeenth birthday, Sam was escorted to a party where she and her date were unquestionably the youngest guests. Jake again was in attendance. Sam, still smarting from his public censure of her activities, set out to provoke him. Up until that time, she had always refused to drink anything stronger than a ginger ale with a squeeze of lemon. But that night she abandoned the self-imposed moral code that had disgruntled many suitors and accepted a Bloody Mary. After finishing the first cocktail, she drank two more, unaware that with each refresher more vodka than tomato juice was being added.

Her date, a member of the university's football team with senior standing, watched her consume the alcohol with great expectations. From across the room, Jake also watched, and he listened. Jake watched her date become more amorous and she more receptive, and listened to her words become more slurred, her laughter more shrill. But he didn't interfere until her date started coaxing her toward the stairs leading to one of the bedrooms. There had been an awful scene with Jake pulling on one arm and telling her that she was leaving, and her date pulling on the other, advising her that Jake wanted her for himself. It was then that Jake lost his temper. He punched her date in the jaw, sending him sprawling on the stairs. Sam's reaction had been violent. She started hitting at Jake, calling him names. Finally, he picked her up, threw her over his shoulder, and took her out of the house, kicking and shrieking all the way. Other guests applauded his action, urging him to give her the spanking she deserved. Sam had screamed all the harder.

Jake had dumped her into the small space that served as the back seat to his sports car, telling her to shut up and lay still each time she started talking incoherent nonsense. At one point she begged him to stop because she was going to be sick. He pulled off the road, lifted her out of the car, and held her while she was violently ill. Afterward he wiped her face with a towel he pulled from a gym bag.

When they reached her home, Sam couldn't find her door key. Since her parents were out of town for the weekend, Jake was forced to retrieve a ladder from his house and crawl through an open upstairs window. While Jake occupied himself with gaining entry into the house, Sam curled up on the front stoop and slept. He awakened her with a gentle shake, and she had giggled and begged him to join her in her icy bed. He told her then that she was a "damned nuisance" and scooped her up in his arms. She had wrapped her arms around Jake's neck as he carried her up the stairs. At the top of the stairs, Jake set her on her own two feet, but when he tried to extricate himself from her hold, she held all the tighter.

Sam could still remember herself telling him not to leave, begging him to kiss her. The memory made her wince. She had wriggled against Jake, pleaded with him to make love to her. He told her she was drunk and didn't understand what she was asking. She told him she did and started kissing him, and when he didn't respond, she began to plead with him.

When the pleading failed, Sam started unbuttoning Jake's shirt, pulling it wide open so she could run her hands over his chest. He pushed her aside roughly when she started kissing his chest, telling her to go to bed and sleep it off. The chide tore at her tender ego and roused her temper.

"No," she told Jake, who by this time had pushed her away. Again he told her to go to bed, but she remained defiant in both words and posture. It was then that Jake's tone of voice became severe, his words cutting.

"You stupid, spoiled little brat," he had called her, "get to bed now or I may give you what you keep asking for."

Sam had responded with a kick to his shins, telling him that he had no right to call her a brat and that she was neither stupid nor spoiled. It was the first time she ever saw Jake get really angry, his startling blue eyes suddenly dark and piercing. He started advancing on her with a deliberation that sent a chill over her body. There had been no other choice but to step back. As he kept advancing, Sam became afraid and began yelling at him to stop. He didn't. He kept coming until she was backed into her bedroom, her legs against the bed. Then he shoved her onto the bed, pinning her arms to her sides.

Slowly he lowered his body onto hers, saying "This is what you wanted, isn't it Sam? To be kissed, to be loved." She had replied with a stammer that she had changed her mind. Jake answered with a kiss that sent a vibration through her entire body. He kept kissing her, and finally, almost involuntarily, she responded. She didn't even offer any resistance when he unbuttoned her blouse and massaged a breast.

Sam began rubbing Jake's back, drawing her nails across the back of his shirt. She called his name over and over, saying yes with each new sensation she felt. When he reached for the zipper of her slacks, she became very frightened and had reached down and gripped one of his wrists as tightly as she could and said, "No, Jake, no." He slapped her hands away and she started crying, saying, "God, Jake, no. I can't. I'm only seventeen. Please." Jake had stopped then. He stood up and adjusted his clothes, his breathing raspy, all the time staring at her. "Next time," he had promised, his voice thick and harsh, "I won't stop." He had left then and Sam had cried herself to sleep. The following morning she made a solemn vow never to tell anyone what had occurred. She never had and never would.

The bath water had grown cold and Sam shivered, but it wasn't the temperature of the water alone that chilled her. It was remembering that Jake's promise of "next time" was just one week away.

Chapter 10

Eyes red and swollen, her emotions still raw, Sam found it very difficult returning to her grandfather's house the next day. She greeted her grandfather as if he were a stranger, cordially and without warmth. As soon as she had collected her purse and phone Sam was ready to leave, anxious to avoid any more dialogue about Jake Sloan.

As expected, her grandfather begged her to stay and talk. Immediately she gave him a feeble excuse about needing time to prepare herself for work the next day. What she really meant was that she needed to reserve her strength for the next morning's meeting with Jake and his promised list of tasks.

Her grandfather persisted with his request for her to remain until Sam agreed. He suggested they retire to the kitchen and Sam shivered as she passed the den, remembering the previous night's events and the final scene with Jake. While her grandfather filled a kettle with water for tea and removed cups and saucers from a cupboard, Sam sat pensively, toying with the strap of her purse. Soon the scent of a newly quartered lemon and the shrill whistle of the kettle pierced the silence in the room. Almost simultaneously, her grandfather handed her a cup of tea and reopened the subject of Jake Sloan with a mumbled apology for his part in persuading her to submit to Jake's demand of marriage.

Devoted as she was to her grandfather, Sam couldn't accept the apology with a gracefully issued obligatory remark. Under different circumstances she would have said "that's all right," or "don't give it another thought," or even, "no apology is necessary." But not this time.

"You knew," Sam accused her grandfather bitterly. "You knew Jake wanted Syntronics and me. Couldn't you have warned me? Prepared me? Shown me the letter before you showed it to Jake?"

Hands circling his teacup, he answered, "If you had been in my position, would you have handled the situation differently?"

"That's not an answer."

"No," acknowledged her grandfather sadly, "It's a defense."

There was a long interval of strained silence before he continued. "I suppose that I, like your father—or perhaps it was Tony who imitated me—didn't have the courage to tell my only grandchild that the legacy from her deceased father was a confession to, if not a criminal act, certainly a wrongful one. I wanted you to mourn the father you loved with only memories you possessed."

Sam fought back the lump that had risen in her throat. "Did you think I would love him less after learning what he had done? Do you love him less?"

"I don't love him any less and don't believe that you ever could. But I think it unpardonably cruel of Tony to have placed the responsibility on his daughter for making amends to the Sloans."

"I don't suppose Dad ever considered the possibility that Jake would exact such a high price."

"He probably didn't."

"I can't help wondering what the future would be like if Dad hadn't left that letter."

"There's one thing I can tell you with certainty."

"What's that?"

"Syntronics would have gone on the auction block."

Samantha wasn't surprised. "I suspected that Dad was having some financial difficulty, but he never said.

"The irony of the situation," commented her grandfather, "is that Jake Sloan is probably one of a few men capable of saving Syntronics. He's a charter member of a very elite business group, figuratively speaking of course, with both the financial resources and the sharp business mind Syntronics desperately needs. There are few other men in the Pacific Northwest—or on the West Coast for that matter—that possess the skills Jake does."

Sam took her first sip of tea and grimaced when she found it bitter and cold. "Okay, so he'll save Syntronics and make a bundle doing it. So why does he have to marry me?"

"You have 40 percent of the stock, my dear."

She didn't entirely grasp his meaning and asked, "Are you telling me and that Jake is marrying me so he'll have one hundred percent control of Syntronics?"

"I believe so."

"Then I'll sell him my stock and be released from this marriage."

His suggestion that Jake wanted marriage only to gain full control of Syntronics had perked up her spirits, but they fell again when he said, "No, dear, you can't."

Sam's face reflected confusion so her grandfather explained, "Under the terms of your father's will—which I assure you is unbreakable and which you should have read in greater detail—you can't sell your stock. Nor can you give it away. The stock can only be bequeathed to your children."

Sam closed her eyes tightly, trying to shut out the prospect of a life with Jake. "So I'll have to go through with this marriage."

"If you want to stop Jake from carrying out his threat to publish the letter, then yes, you will."

"Do you really think he would? Publish the letter I mean."

"Do you?"

It took her only a second to answer, "Yes." Jake didn't make idle threats.

"Sam, Jake may be a hard man, but he's an honest one. And he's fair." She knew the message her grandfather intended was that Jake had given his word that he would not publish the letter if she married him and her grandfather believed Jake to be an honorable man, one that lived by his promises.

Sam pondered her grandfather's assessment of Jake and then presented her own. "Jake certainly is hard, honest, and I suppose, fair. He's also overbearing, dictatorial, arrogant, and vindictive." She could have added more colorful adjectives to the list, but didn't.

Her grandfather gave her a searching, speculative look before responding to her acidic remarks. "I think you should try to purge all this hostility and anger you hold toward Jake before you become his wife."

The words of caution had no effect. "My thoughts and feelings may be the only things he won't be able to control."

"Oh, Sam," her grandfather appeared modestly alarmed, "don't invite more disaster in your life. If you oppose Jake, that's exactly what you'll be doing. Make no mistake that Jake is a man. A man's man. He's not like the young men...boys really...that you've dated. He won't tolerate your demand for total independence and he won't accept rebellion, no matter how it's disguised."

"I won't reshape my life or my personality to suit Jake Sloan!"

"Then I suggest you prepare yourself for a very rocky relationship," he proclaimed gravely. "And don't ask me to rescue you, Sam. Your father and mother handled their differences privately and I'll expect you to do the same."

Stunned by his pronouncement, Sam said, "I can't believe you intend to abandon me after I'm married to Jake."

"I didn't say I was going to abandon you. I said that I wasn't going to interfere."

"It isn't as though I'm in love with the man. He's a virtual stranger to me!"

"Just as I was to your grandmother. Oh, don't look so surprised. Our marriage started out as one of convenience.

And don't ask me why because it's none of your business." His voice took on a gentler quality when he spoke of his late wife. "Sometime during our first year, we fell in love. But in the beginning, we were strangers and I can tell you that there were many subjects and many issues on which your grandmother and I disagreed. But we worked it out, just as you and Jake will work it out."

Not for one minute did Sam believe that she and Jake would "work it out."

"Don't you think the very basis for this marriage negates any possibility that it will survive? This isn't convenience, it's me being his indentured servant."

"After this coming Saturday the reason for the marriage isn't going to be relevant any longer. The marriage in reality will exist and you'll be obligated to conduct yourself as a married woman."

"Granddad," Sam sputtered in extreme frustration, "I really can't believe we're having this conversation. Twenty minutes ago you were telling me you were sorry for urging me to marry Jake and, in so many words, that it was unjust that I must pay the penalty for my father's actions. Now, in complete contradictory fashion, you sound as though you support this marriage, which completely...baffles me. For pity's sake, Jake Sloan will be my keeper. He'll try to tell me how I can think, what I can say, what I can do."

Her grandfather stubbornly maintained his position. "Sam, you made a commitment last night to marry Jake. I expect you to fulfill that commitment regardless of the reason it was given. And having made that commitment, I think you should deal with the reality of the situation. Jake will be your husband, not your jailer."

"In my case it's one in the same."

"If you truly believe that, then call Jake now and tell him you can't go through with the marriage." He pointed to the phone for emphasis. Sam looked at the phone and was sorely tempted to do as he suggested. She hung her head and said, "He'll publish the letter. I couldn't bear that." She looked up at her grandfather then. "I suppose that makes me weak, too."

"Just proud, Sam. Just proud."

The old adage of pride coming before a fall popped into her mind. "So, we're back to the beginning, or should I say the end. I marry Jake, I save Daddy's name, and save the company. Who's going to save me?"

Her grandfather gave her a sympathetic look, but never answered her question. Finally, he rose from his chair and put the kettle back on the burner. It was his way of ending a conversation. From experience Sam knew he had said all he was going to about the subject and would say no more. In resignation, she just sat and waited for another cup of tea.

Chapter 11

Monday morning Jake handed her a list of things to do that was twenty items long. She scanned the list and noted with amazement that he had missed few details. He had prioritized what needed to be accomplished for the wedding, indicating the most important tasks as having blood tests and getting a marriage license. These tasks, he indicated, were to be done that afternoon.

Without asking for her concurrence, he gave her a verbal agenda for the day, starting with a visit to a local physician for all the important blood tests, followed by a quiet lunch at a local restaurant in Bellevue. Afterwards, he said, they would contact a local magistrate, and then travel to Seattle to choose a ring.

At lunch, Jake didn't even permit Sam the option of selecting her own lunch. His proprietary attitude enraged her so much that heated words passed between them. From there the afternoon deteriorated. They disagreed on the magistrate, fought over what pose was best for an engagement picture. Jake, brusque and authoritative, managed to win every dispute, which angered Sam even more.

By the time they reached the jewelers, it was quite clear to Sam that Jake intended to choreograph every detail of the impending ceremony without soliciting her opinion—not that she was particularly bothered by the fact, though there were certain details she thought should be left to her discretion alone. She didn't want to contribute any more effort than was absolutely necessary to becoming Mrs. Jake Sloan.

In a secluded corner of a very exclusive jeweler in downtown Seattle, Jake gave a detailed description of the engagement ring he wanted for her. Inwardly smoldering at Jake's behavior and his total lack of consideration, Sam decided to select a ring completely contrary to the one he described. Tray after tray of beautifully crafted rings, most with diamonds three carat and larger, were displayed for her. With a whimsical wave of her hand she rejected each as unsuitable.

Jake and the middle-aged jeweler were equally frustrated, though the jeweler concealed his feelings better than Jake. Ire fairly emanated from Jake. When the soft-spoken jeweler excused himself to retrieve yet another display tray from a vault, Jake delivered an ultimatum. Out of the corner of his mouth he snarled, "Choose. Or I'll choose for you."

Sam bit back the retort that sprang to her lips. Telling Jake flatly it wasn't her idea to be there in the first place would have led to a public confrontation, which eventually would have led to private retribution. So, she remained silent and waited for the jeweler to return.

She smiled out of courtesy as yet another velvet-covered tray was set before her. Sam viewed the selection with as little interest as she had the six trays before. In the last row though, she spied a two carat diamond solitaire. She asked to see it and the jeweler slipped it on her finger. Sam studied the ring from different angles; the size of the gem and the simplistic style of the ring appealed to her. It was also the ring farthest in appearance from what Jake wanted.

"This one," she said to Jake and heard the jeweler expel a long sigh.

"Are you sure?" questioned Jake, as he looked at the ring. "It's very small." He wore a square-cut, two karat diamond ring on the smallest finger of his right hand.

"Quite sure," she said without inflection. Jake frowned and the jeweler beamed.

"And the bands?"

Sam glanced at the brushed gold bands, and shrugged. "They're fine." There was no enthusiasm in her voice or in her manner.

She tried to pull off the ring but a scowling Jake grabbed her hand, saying "You'll wear it." He pushed the ring back in place.

Alone that evening, Sam debated on whether or not to call Jill and tell her about the forthcoming marriage before Jill read about it on the Web. Finally, she decided it was best to deliver the news first hand. Sam telephoned and invited John and Jill to meet her at the Velvet Turtle in Bellevue for a drink.

Pulling into the parking lot of the popular night spot for young professionals, Sam found a vacant space not far from where the Simms' vehicle was parked. She stood conspicuously in the entrance leading to the lounge, scanning the semi-darkened room for her friends. On her second sweep of the room, she spotted Jill hailing her with a waving hand from a corner table.

Sam passed through the room without much difficulty, pausing a few times to speak with people whom she hadn't seen in a while. As she approached the Simms, John stood and pulled out a chair. Jill and Sam exchanged greetings while John motioned for the waitress.

"Well," Jill said happily as Sam settled more comfortably into the chair, "it's been a long time since we all shared a relaxing evening together."

A smiling John agreed, "It certainly has."

He and Jill were holding hands. Sam, her own hands hidden in her lap to conceal the engagement ring, marveled at how they appeared more like young lovers than a comfortably married couple.

With heartfelt sincerity Sam said, "I'm really glad you both could join me." The waitress returned with a tray of drinks. John played the gentleman and dismissed Sam's offer to pay and withdrew several bills from his wallet.

"How was dinner with your grandfather?" Knowing Jill as well as she did, Sam had anticipated the question, and had prepared an answer.

"Absolutely wonderful," she enthused between sips of her drink. "His explanation of Jake's control of Syntronics was quite satisfactory." To lend credibility to the story, Sam wore an artificial smile.

"What was the explanation?" The question came from John.

"It was just as you thought, John," she maintained the false gaiety, "Grandfather, after consulting with several financial experts on the state of affairs at Syntronics, determined that someone with an entrepreneurial spirit—and "with grit," his words, was needed to save the company from financial disaster. Jake was the best candidate." John at least accepted the falsehood as true. Jill didn't appear as convinced.

"See," John boasted to Jill, his ego swelling, "I knew I was right." Jill, with appropriate wifely restraint, didn't contradict him, but she gave Sam a conspiratorial wink.

"There's something else I need to tell you both." The Simms gave Sam their full attention. She had rehearsed how she was going to present the news of her impending marriage over and over again in the car. She delivered the news in one short breath. "I'm getting married."

Jill gasped, "I don't believe it."

"It's true." Sam flashed the engagement ring. John held up the candle so he could see the gem more clearly, then let out a low whistle, saying, "That set someone back a penny or two."

"I don't believe it," Jill repeated, dropping back in her chair. "Samantha Ward getting married! You're the girl who declared on graduation day she was dedicating her life to a career, not a man." Then with suspicion she asked, "Who is it you're planning to marry anyway? So far as I know you haven't even had a steady relationship with anyone since..." Jill stopped mid-sentence and gave Sam a long, speculative stare, then muttered, "No."

"Yes," confirmed Sam, sensing that Jill had guessed.

John, aware that he had missed some crucial piece of information in the conversation, demanded of Jill, "Who is it she hasn't had a relationship with in a long time?"

Jill nudged him. "Ask her. Go ahead. Ask her who she's going to marry."

"Okay," John obliged. "Who's the lucky fellow, Sam."

"Jake Sloan." Sam emptied her glass.

John's reaction was comical. His mouth dropped open and stayed in that position until his wife reached out a hand and gently pushed his chin upward.

A shocked John asked, "Is this what you want, Sam?" She knew he was thinking of her admission the week before that she didn't even like Jake. And she was just as confident that Jill thought that Sam and Jake had been lovers at one time.

"Let's just say," she said cryptically, "that Jake made me an offer I couldn't refuse." It was trite, but as honest an answer as she dared provide. She hated to lie outright and half-truths weren't much better.

John, about to comment on Sam's remark, was silenced by Jill quietly placing a hand on his arm. "Darling, we're forgetting to congratulate Sam," the reproof was given gently. In unison, they extended their congratulations and followed it with a toast to her future happiness.

"When is the wedding?" inquired Jill, finishing her drink.

"This Saturday," Sam mumbled, glad the lighting was subdued enough to cloak her facial expression.

Jill's eyes flew open, John's head jerked forward as if he hadn't heard her quite right.

"Saturday?" Jill leaned heavily on the small table in an effort to see Sam better. Her eyes were narrowed and watchful.

Before Jill had time to form a question, Sam spoke. "You'll both come, of course."

"Of course," John responded for both of them.

"I'll have to give you the details about time and place by Wednesday," explained Sam. "It won't be a church wedding. Just a very small civil ceremony"

Again Jill gave her a curious look. "And the ceremony is Saturday?"

"Yes," Sam confirmed, wishing Jill would let the subject drop, but knowing she wouldn't.

Jill didn't, "Why the rush?"

"Jake thinks the marriage will provide a little more security to the business community—bankers in particular—that Syntronics is here to stay. I guess you can look at the marriage as sort of a business partnership designed to quiet all the rumors that have been flying since Jake took over."

Jill continued to push the issue. "So this marriage is merely a business arrangement. Is that what you're saying?"

She knew how Jake would have responded. His answer would have been "absolutely not." She could almost hear him saying it. But Jake wasn't there. Samantha side-stepped the question as best she could. "I suppose it depends on your perspective. Syntronics has a great future now that Jake is in charge."

"And what's your perspective?" Jill fired back at her. John sat passively listening to the conversation, looking from one girl to the other.

Sam was getting tense. "My perspective? Well, I guess," she struggled for a convincing answer, "Well, it's...it's a business arrangement."

Jill wasn't satisfied. "Come on, Sam, let's go check our makeup." Sam instantly recognized Jill's suggestion as a flimsy excuse to get Sam alone so that Jill could browbeat her as she had on other occasions when Sam was reluctant to reveal all about a situation.

John told Jill her makeup looked just fine. "Thank you, dear, but I want to check my hair."

Trying to avoid the private interview with Jill, Sam said, "Go ahead Jill, I'll stay here with John."

"I want some company," insisted Jill.

There was a determination in Jill's stance. Reluctantly, Sam joined her. No sooner had they entered the woman's restroom than Jill started her interrogation.

"What's going on?" Jill asked bluntly.

"Nothing," Sam retorted lightly, removing a brush from her purse.

Jill crossed her arms and leaned against the counter. "Don't tell me nothing is going on. A week ago you were practically foaming at the mouth because Jake Sloan was at Syntronics. Now you're going to marry him in less than a week and you tell me that *nothing* is going on. You may be able to fool my husband, but you can't fool me."

Sam continued brushing her hair, trying to appear nonchalant. "I told you. It's a business arrangement."

Jill wasn't buying her act. "I know what you said and we both know you're telling a story."

"No, I'm not," denied Sam coolly, applying fresh lipstick she didn't really need.

"Oh, yes you are," Jill charged. "I've always been able to tell when you're lying or when you're holding something back. Take last week, for instance. There's more between you and Jake than Syntronics."

"Do you know all my secrets?" She snapped her purse closed.

"No," admitted Jill frankly. "I don't. But I do have to assure myself that you're all right."

"I am," Sam told her stubbornly. "So, put on lipstick or something and let's have another drink."

Jill peered at her image in the mirror. "John's right. My makeup is perfect." Sam laughed. It really was impossible to be annoyed with Jill for very long.

As they left the restroom, Jill put out a hand to delay Sam. "Listen, my friend. It's obvious, at least to me, that you're not as happy about this marriage as you pretend. No, let me finish. And I'll quit pestering you, though I really don't want to. So compromise, will you. I promise not to ask you any more questions if you'll promise me one thing."

"If I can," started Sam cautiously, not knowing what kind of promise Jill was attempting to extract from her.

"Promise me that you'll call me if things get too rough."

"I'll be fine," Sam tried to sound more reassuring than she felt.

"Sure you will," said Jill doubtfully. "But if you aren't, please," she implored, "call."

"I promise."

Jill smiled. "Good. Now I'm ready for that second drink."

Chapter 12

Samantha resisted a temptation to call in ill the next morning, not because it had been late when she had returned home from the Velvet Turtle, and not because she had a hangover. She simply wanted a quiet, peaceful day; a day without any confrontations with Jake.

In the end, plagued by a guilty conscience and a strong work ethic, she went to work. On reaching the office she was sorry she hadn't made the call. Jake, looking more formidable than usual, met her at the elevator door.

"Come with me," he ordered a startled Sam, barely giving her enough time to step out of the elevator before he took hold of her arm.

Fortunately, most of the employees were still consuming their first cup of coffee in the employees lounge so there was no one to observe Jake marching Sam down the hallway at a brisk pace to his office. His stride was so much longer than hers she found herself running to keep in step with him. Since he had such a firm hold on her upper arm, there was little else she could do.

Carol, still putting away some personal items in a desk drawer, looked up in astonishment as Jake whipped by and propelled Sam into his office. Before slamming the door shut with a bang, he told Carol to hold all his calls. Sam stood tensely in the center of the office, wondering what in the world had sent his blood pressure soaring this time.

Jake, hands on hip, suit jacket flung back, was very agitated. "Where the hell were you last night?"

Sam stared at him blankly, not quite comprehending the question. Then she remembered her cell phone had been ringing when she was entering the house last night. She had accidentally left the phone behind when she went to meet Jill and John. When she picked up the phone, she didn't recognize the number and decided to ignore the call. And then she turned off the phone. At the time, she recalled wondering who could have been calling her at such a late hour. Now she knew.

"I was out." Sam said matter-of-factly, adjusting the shoulder strap of her purse.

"I asked you a question," Jake bellowed and for a second Sam's imagination took control and she pictured thin columns of steam spewing out of his nostrils.

She vanquished the image and with bravado replied, "And I answered you."

"Don't," a long finger was pointed swiftly at her, "hedge. When I ask you a question, I expect a straight answer."

Sam chewed on her bottom lip, experiencing the first pangs of nervousness with the encounter. Is this what life was to be like with him she wondered. "I did answer you. I was out."

Jake pursed his lips, and then said threateningly, "You want to play games with me, Sam? You think you can win?"

Goosebumps covered her whole body, she swallowed hard. "Which question do you want me to answer?"

Eyebrows raised, his voice curiously restrained, Jake said "So it's to be games, is it."

Samantha felt the knot in her stomach twist painfully. "I didn't say that."

"You haven't said anything yet," there was a grating edge to his voice. "I'm going to ask you one more time. Where were you last night?"

She shifted her weight from one side to the other. "At the Velvet Turtle."

"With?" He asked testily.

"The Simms." He made her feel like a child who had to account for her activities away from home.

"Who else?"

"No one."

He didn't say anything for some minutes. "Did you tell the Simms about the wedding?"

"Yes."

"And what else did you tell them?"

"Nothing," she responded, thinking he was referring to her father's letter.

"Nothing?" Jake wasn't assured.

"Nothing," Sam repeated.

"What reason did you give them for our marrying so quickly?"

She knew he wasn't going to like her answer. "I told them it was a business arrangement." He reacted more violently than she anticipated.

"You what?" Jake shouted loudly and Samantha cowered under his hostile gaze.

"I could...couldn't tell them the truth," she stammered in her own defense. "The Simms would never tell anyone what I said."

The answer was like waving a red flag in front of a bull. "My concern isn't with the Simms, it's with you."

Bewildered by his statement, Sam said, "I don't know what you mean."

"Telling others," he told her viciously, "that our marriage is to be a business relationship is pure fantasy. You're perpetuating a fallacy in your own little mind. I told you Saturday there would be no closed doors between us and I meant it."

"Fine," Sam said recklessly. "From now on when anyone inquiries about my impending marriage to you I'll explain you're an extortionist and forcing me into a marriage I don't want."

It was the wrong thing to say. Two large hands descended on her shoulders and Sam shrieked. Jake, his face as dark as midnight, shook her. Before she had time to recover, he crushed his lips to hers in a hard punishing kiss, stifling her protests. Her whole body twisted in response to his assault, trying to break free.

His hands slowly worked their way from her shoulders to the back of her head, his fingers entwined in her hair.

Gradually the kiss turned tender and she quit struggling against him and found herself welcoming the soft and gentle pressure of his lips.

When Jake released her abruptly, she fell back into a chair, clinging to its steel arms, shaken by the intensity of his emotions, frightened by her own. Her breathing was shallow, her face drained of all color.

She refused to relinquish her slouched position in the chair, even when Jake told her to do so, "Straighten up, Sam."

More interested in restoring her breathing to a normal pattern than in bowing to Jake's wishes, Sam said between clenched teeth, "Leave me alone."

He bent to help her to a sitting position and Sam struck at his arms with all the might she could muster.

"Don't touch me," she rasped and Jake shoved his hands in his pockets.

"Look, Sam," he gazed down at his shoes, "I'm sorry I lost my temper. I admit that I have a short fuse, especially where you're concerned."

Smoothing out her crumpled coat, Samantha said bitterly, "Sorry isn't good enough. You're an adult and should have more control over your emotions. I didn't make you angry. You made yourself angry. Yet, you punish me because you want the situation to be as you dictate it, not as it really is."

Drawing a deep breath she continued, "I'm not accustomed to having to account for my time to anyone. You make all these demands on me and I'm supposed to say, yes, master, anything you want, master. And what about me, Jake? What do I get out of this relationship? So far, just admonishments and punishments. I didn't deserve to be shaken like a rag doll. And then you kissed me as if...as if...you owned me! All right, so I lied to the Simms. Jill was needling me about the reason I was marrying you. At the time, I simply couldn't think of any other explanation."

The hands came out of his pockets as he moved over to his desk. Sam wasn't surprised to see them balled into tight fists. Sitting down in the huge leather chair, he said, "Okay, Sam, what do you want?"

Despite the ring of sincerity of his voice, she looked at him with distrust. "I want you to quit bullying me, Jake."

"Then start obeying me," he countered, "and stop antagonizing me."

"It's not too difficult to antagonize someone with a low-boiling point like yours," Sam sniffed, waiting for another blast of temper from Jake that never arrived.

Jake, now fully in charge of his emotions, said calmly, "When the person is deliberately trying to push all the right buttons, no it isn't."

"And I suppose I'm the one who is pushing all the right buttons," she said sarcastically, miffed by his insinuation.

"Yes," he cocked his head to one side and a lock of hair fell on his forehead, making him look rather boyish, "just like you did this morning. All you had to do was answer my question."

"Your demand," corrected Sam.

"Don't you think I have the right as your fiancé to know where you spend your evenings?"

Samantha told him "No," and Jake stated, "And I suppose you also think that after you're my wife you still won't have to explain your whereabouts to me?"

"That's right," Sam replied, now totally composed.

"That's wrong," he said with conviction.

Sam challenged him, "Why is that wrong? What gives you the right to impose restraints on my life?"

"As your husband," he informed her casually as he loosened his tie, "I have the right to establish certain rules in our marriage."

"Rubbish," declared Sam hotly. "Your concept of marriage is archaic and indicative of a masochistic personality."

"I'm not going to change."

"And neither am I," she explained.

"More the pity for you, Sam," commented Jake.

"Why pity?"

He leaned forward in his chair and issued a warning with a smile. "Because you haven't enough sense to know when to stop. You'll defy me, bait me, and push me, and you'll suffer the consequences of your actions."

Unperturbed by the implied threat, Sam stood her ground. "I refuse to alter my lifestyle because it conflicts with yours."

His hands opened expressively in a gesture of resignation. "Then you'll suffer the consequences." Frustrated by his implacability, Sam found it impossible to maintain a cool reserve. "Consequences! Always consequences. No compromises, no negotiations, no discussions. Jake's law! I'll choke on it!"

"Then you'll choke," promised Jake, unmoved by her impassioned words. "I told you before. And I'm getting tired of telling you. I'm in charge."

She found his reference to himself as being in charge, which in her mind amounted to saying he was her master, intolerable. "Why," she implored, "can't you be reasonable? Why is it all black and white? This way—your way—or no way."

"We've already covered that territory." Anger was slowly creeping into his voice again. "I'm going to tell you one last time, and you damn well better not bring up the subject again, that as your husband I'll determine how you'll live."

"Jake…"

"Enough, Sam."

"If you'd only…"

"Enough."

"…listen to reason. Surely…"

She was interrupted by Jake's fist hitting the desk with such a force that a small stack of papers just at the very edge of the desk were sent flying to the floor. Even she jerked back in surprise. Sam met his hostile gaze for as long as she could, trying earnestly to convey a mute message to Jake that she was a free and independent spirit who was not going to accept the shackles of marriage gracefully. But it was she who blinked first, and she who finally looked away. In the few minutes of the exchange, she resurrected a plan she had been toying with for days, but one she had just the night before discarded as foolish. A plan, which she believed, if successful, would clearly demonstrate to Jake she had no intention of being ruled by him.

Further conversation was prevented when Carol rapped loudly on the door and then entered with an apology for having interrupted their meeting. When Jake asked what it was she wanted, Carol's eyes darted from one to the other, finally settling with Jake. Then she said, with unmistakable skepticism, "There's a reporter, actually, a photographer, here. From the *Times*. He said he's here to take a picture of you and Miss Ward." Carol paused and looked questionably at Sam. "He said they'd greatly appreciate having an exclusive picture of you and your…your fiancé."

Jake glanced at Sam and told Carol, "Give us five minutes and then escort the photographer in, please."

As Carol turned away to leave, Jake called her back. "By the way, Carol, I'm sorry you had to learn the news from someone else. Sam and I had hoped to tell you the happy news ourselves."

"Then it's true," Carol couldn't keep the note of incredulity from her voice, but added warmly, "My congratulations to you both."

Sam responded with, "Thank you, Carol. The wedding is Saturday and you, of course, are invited. It will be a small private ceremony, but Jake has insisted on a large reception. I hope you'll attend."

Carol said she wouldn't think of missing it and then exited. Jake waited until the door lock had clicked and turned to Sam. "Please. Smiles and affection."

"But of course," Sam responded sarcastically, already searching for her cosmetic bag to repair her damaged makeup.

When the photographer entered, Sam and Jake were standing together. Carol made the introductions and lingered while the photographer looked about the room to choose an appropriate background for the shot. Sam was grateful the photographer was experienced and quick. She didn't want to be close to Jake for any longer than absolutely necessary. Ten minutes later she was alone with him again.

Snatching up the coat she had discarded for the picture, Sam said, "I guess I can go to work now."

"Yes," said Jake, "but please don't make any appointments for later this afternoon."

Her shoulders dropped, as if weighted down by a heavy burden. "Why not?"

"Because I would like to show you your new home."

Sam sighed audibly. She had no desire whatsoever to see Jake's house. "What time?"

"Four o'clock."

"Shall I come to your office or will you come to mine?"

"Why don't we meet halfway," suggested Jake with amusement.

Sam wasn't amused and told him, "I'll meet you at the elevator."

Chapter 13

Concentrating on the SALCOMP project proved to be difficult. Instead of keeping her attention on the placement of commas and semicolons in the text she was reviewing, she thought about Jake's excessive anger toward her. His displays of temper seemed extreme and frequently out of proportion to the crime.

His price for revenge was marriage, and she had already agreed to this demand, so why was he intimidating and humiliating her at every opportunity. The demonstration of his displeasure with her earlier in his office had been the worst episode to date and, just for a moment, when he had first started his inquisition, she had actually thought he was showing signs of jealousy.

After a mental debate, she decided this was a ludicrous idea. After all, their paths had crossed infrequently over the last seven years or so. There had been several social functions at which both had been guests, but they had never exchanged more than a nodding hello.

Jake had always openly appraised her escorts, and she had regarded his dates with interest. Never once, however, had either made a move to draw the other into conversation. But still, there had always been something indefinable—a look, a feeling—that passed between them on those occasions. After a while, Sam quit trying to find an explanation for the inexplicable. It wasn't until her evening last week with Jill that Sam had even considered that the indefinable was in fact a strong physical attraction between them.

When she wasn't trying to make sense of Jake's violence and his kisses, she was busy formulating the details of her escape plan. By the time the scheduled rendezvous with Jake arrived, she hadn't progressed beyond the first paragraph of text she had begun reviewing hours before.

Sam was putting away the project files when the company's young receptionist entered. As usual, Karen sounded quite breathless when asking, "Is it true?"

"Is what true?" Sam asked, clearing off the rest of her desk.

"Are you marrying him?" Karen's emphasis on the pronoun amused Sam. Karen frequently used the same tone to describe a particularly undesirable neighbor who had aspirations of being a suitor.

"Yes," Sam retorted, "I'm marrying him." Karen's face fell.

"Gees Louise," commented the girl absently. "And I told Sue in accounting that it couldn't be true."

"Well, it is." Sam put on her coat and adjusted the collar.

Karen said "Wow" and Sam asked, "Am I to interpret that as congratulations?"

"What? Oh, yes, congratulations!" Karen didn't give the impression that the news was worth congratulating.

"Thank you. Now, I have to meet Jake, so let's hurry."

Jake was standing impatiently in front of the elevator, consulting his watch every few seconds. When he saw Sam and Karen approaching, he smiled. Karen, still impressed by Jake's charismatic manner, beamed at him.

"Hello, Mr. Sloan," Karen said too sweetly, taking her place at her desk. The girl's manner reminded Sam of a new puppy she once had that stuck to her like glue.

"Good afternoon, Karen," Jake responded politely, pressing the down button of the elevator.

"Oh, Mr. Sloan. Congratulations to you and Sam, I mean Ms. Ward."

Karen's remark caused Jake to cast a look of suspicion in Sam's direction. Sam answered his unspoken question. "It seems most everyone knows about the wedding plans."

Jake smiled graciously at Karen. "Thank you, Karen."

Karen was still bestowing a look of adoration upon Jake as the elevator doors closed.

As they descended to the garage level, Jake asked, "Is Karen always like that?"

"Like what?"

"She always appears...preoccupied."

"It's a state of mind that seems to occur mainly in your presence," commented Sam.

Jake appeared puzzled by her explanation for a brief interval and then he comprehended the statement. "Oh. I see."

There was no more conversation between them until Jake turned the car into an older and more exclusive subdivision on the southwest shore of Lake Washington.

"I didn't know you lived so close to the office," remarked Sam. She had pictured Jake living in a flashy penthouse apartment in one of the more exclusive, high-rise residential establishments in downtown Seattle.

"I had the house built three years ago," Jake told her, as he drove down a driveway nearly hidden by towering evergreens. The asphalt driveway appeared to end at a massive wooden wall, at least two stories high and the width of three garages, studded at each end by columns of large rocks. Jake stopped just short of the wall, pressed a button on a small square box attached to his windshield visor, and a huge garage door swung open.

Sam exclaimed in surprise. "No one would ever know that the door is there."

"That's the idea," Jake informed her with a slightly sarcastic tone.

He parked the car and said, "Let me give you a tour of the grounds first."

The grounds and the house were quite unlike any she had seen before in the vicinity. Clearly a custom design, the two-story structure was banked by a small grove of trees at the rear and a sloping lawn at the front and was surrounded by a wide variety of shrubbery and flowering plants. A cobbled path skirted the east side of the house and led to a dock where a sailboat was moored. The entire front of the house was glass. Jake told her the design was based on the shape of a crescent moon and that the structure was really two houses in one.

Because the upper level extended over the garage, it was much larger than the lower level, and the third level served as an oversized patio. The lower level, Jake explained, was used strictly for entertaining. When Sam saw the area she understood why.

It was a large, open space, which had clearly been professionally decorated. Sam found the effect attractive, but impersonal. She realized that the room was specifically designed to impress but not to reveal anything about its owner.

As Jake escorted her toward the wide staircase leading to the upper level, he gave his reasons for separating his living space from his entertaining space. Sam wasn't at all surprised to hear him say that he didn't like invasions of his privacy, nor to hear him tell her that a professional image didn't always equate with personal comfort.

At the stairs leading to the upper level of the house, Jake made an excuse about checking something in the garage and left Sam to explore on her own. She wandered at leisure, pausing briefly in each room, some of which were furnished, and some of which were not. So far she had seen three bedrooms, a dining area, a kitchen, and a living room.

The ambience of the upper level differed greatly from the lower. Here she found warm, comfortable surroundings. Jake had chosen furnishings and accents that blended perfectly. Even the color schemes were perfect—rich blues and pastel yellows—making the rooms seem alive and inviting. The whole effect was pleasing to her.

She lingered in a room that was obviously Jake's domain, a medium-sized office tucked in a corner with a view of the lake. Nowhere was Jake's personality more in evidence than in here.

Every wall was covered with an assortment of photographs, some small, some large, some black and white, and some in color.

She recognized his father and mother in several, both smiling lovingly at each other as if there was no audience. There were many of Jake and his father. In one photograph the two male Sloans were in a sailboat. In another they were at the stadium watching a baseball game, and then there was a shot of both seated at Emerald Downs, the racetrack. There was even a photograph of Jake and his father atop Mount Rainier. Then there were many pictures of Mr. Sloan alone. From the collection of photographs, it would be apparent to even a stranger that the Sloans shared a strong bond of love.

Samantha was about to withdraw from the room, a trifle discomforted by having intruded on what was so clearly a private sanctum for treasured memories, when she saw what she thought to be a picture of herself almost hidden behind a stack of papers on the desk. She glanced over her shoulder to ensure she was still alone, then reached behind the papers and picked up the small frame, surprised to find that she was indeed the girl in the picture, at the same time trying to recall when the photo had been taken. She stretched her mind, but couldn't remember. She knew it had to be from her college days because she hadn't worn her hair in that particular style since her senior year at the university. The biggest question she had was why Jake would have a picture of her in his home. One idea sprang to mind, but she dismissed it as utterly preposterous. She carefully returned the picture to its resting place, readjusting the papers. With a final look about the room, she left, taking with her a feeling of uneasiness.

The room immediately to the right of Jake's den increased her uneasiness. It was the master bedroom. She hardly noticed the layout of the room, her attention drawn to the single furnishing that dominated the room—a king-size bed. The sight of the bed conjured up a vision that she found very disturbing. She left hastily, deciding it was time to seek out Jake, only to encounter him on the stairs. Although there was more than ample width for three people to ascend the stairs abreast, Jake chose to ignore this fact and stood very close to her.

"Did you see the master bedroom?" he asked pointedly.

"I saw it." She averted her eyes, suddenly finding a landscape painting on the wall of great interest.

"And what do you think?" Jake probed.

Sam didn't want to tell him she had done no more than glance at the room. Nor did she want him to know she had taken one look at the king-size bed from the open doorway and had looked no further. She gave Jake a noncommittal answer. "It's okay."

He reached out for her hand and then tucked it into the crook of his arm, "Let me show it to you properly."

"I've seen it, Jake," she said stubbornly, pulling away from him. She rubbed her hand briskly where he had held it, trying to erase his touch.

Jake, standing on the step above, looked down at her and said, "But I'd like you to see it again."

Sam knew if she didn't yield to his request there would be another battle. "Okay, Jake. Let's look at the master bedroom."

She gestured for him to lead the way.

On closer inspection, Sam realized the room was quite large, with his and her dressing quarters and baths at opposite sides. Pretending interest, she walked into the ample closet space that adjoined the bath area with the more feminine décor.

"Will this area be large enough for your clothes?" Jake enquired from somewhere behind her.

She ran a hand over a shelf as if she were measuring its depth. "Yes it will, and then some."

"Good. I made arrangements this afternoon for a moving company to relocate your household furnishings and personal belongings here on Friday.

Sam spun around and responded angrily, "You had no right to do that!"

Jake, blocking the exit from the closet, raised an eyebrow, "Didn't I?"

"No. You didn't." She tried to sweep past him, but his arms came up and barred the way. "I'd like to pass, please."

Jake flashed one of his famous smiles and said with a suggestive air, "I like you just where you are."

Sam could tell Jake had no intention of moving and immediately became defensive. "I don't know what you mean."

"I know you don't, Sam. That's what makes it so much fun. And so interesting." The smile was even broader.

It was easy to see that Jake was thoroughly enjoying her discomfort, because he was being very cocky.

Exasperated by what she considered to be a deterioration in the conversation, Sam asked crisply, "What are you talking about?"

"Ask me," suggested Jake.

"Ask you what?"

"To let you by."

"I already have."

"Try a different approach."

Sam looked at Jake more keenly, sure that he was leading the conversation to an end where she again would emerge his victim. Still, she was curious.

"And just what do you suggest, Jake?"

His arms dropped and he propped himself against the door jamb. A mischievous glint was in his eyes.

"I'm so glad you asked, Sam, because I happen to be a certified master of the soft approach."

The disclosure, made in a teasing manner, sufficiently convinced Sam that Jake was drawing her into his web, but she continued to play along, adopting a light-hearted approach. "Okay, Jake, I'll bite. Am I to sink to my knees and beg your pardon and humbly request permission to pass or am I just to beg?"

He straightened and acted visibly wounded by her suggestion, "Sam, you accuse me unjustly. I'm merely suggesting, my dear, that you use some of your feminine charm in this situation. After all, you must admit that it's something I've not been privileged to see since our...reunion."

Sam cringed at his bold suggestion. "Sorry, I seem to have misplaced my charm."

"I'm sure if you try hard enough you'll find it."

"But I don't want to find it."

"But I do." Jake moved toward her.

With her back against the wall, her purse clutched to her breasts, Sam was a prime target for Jake. He took four steps and was in front of her. Her body went rigid as he placed his hands gently on her shoulders and drew her towards him.

"I think you need a lesson in being a woman, Sam. You've become too aggressive and definitely too independent."

Sam said rather nastily, her chin elevated, "No one else has ever complained."

"I'm not surprised. I've seen the men you date, Sam," he said with derision. He then reached out and cupped her face with his hands and traced the outline of her lips with his thumbs. "All boys. All weak. All easily controlled by and dominated by a woman with more self-assurance than they possess. I'm not a boy."

He lowered his mouth to hers. The kiss was not unexpected, but the pleasure she derived from it was. It was warm and tender and searching, and she found herself responding. Jake. Feeling her response, he embraced her more tightly, and the kiss deepened. As a desire to embrace Jake grew within her, Sam had to forcibly disengage her charged emotions and to command herself to break away from Jake's passionate hold.

She stood self-consciously before him, her cheeks deeply flushed, embarrassed because she had allowed him to possess her, even if it was for mere minutes. Jake's face was beside hers and she could hear and feel his short and shallow breaths.

His hand came up to softly stroke her cheek and she turned her head away and asked him to stop.

"Why?" he whispered in her ear. "You're enjoying it."

"Because...oh...just stop," she stammered as he continued the caress.

Jake stopped and braced his arms against the wall, trapping her in between. "Why do you insist on denying the physical attraction between us? And don't tell me you don't know what I'm talking about, because you damn well do."

Sam couldn't look him in the eye. The question caught her off-guard. If she admitted that she did recognize that a physical attraction existed between them, Jake would resume his advances. If she tried to deny the attraction, he would become perturbed and, she suspected, extremely angry. In either case she knew she couldn't win. Whatever she said would irritate Jake.

With a sigh she chose what she believed to be the least painful route and said, "Okay. So there's a physical attraction. It's insignificant."

"It's insignificant?" Jake repeated without any sign of humor. "To whom?"

Sam tried to minimize the impact the impact of her previous statement with a shrug and a flimsy retraction. "Insignificant isn't exactly what I meant."

Jake was watching her closely; a muscle was pulsating in his jaw. His bad temper had returned.

"It's what you said."

"Yes, I know, but...well...okay, there's definitely a physical attraction. Are you satisfied?" she snapped.

"Not quite," announced Jake as he pulled her back into his arms and kissed her until her body went slack. She was gasping for air as he let her go. "Now I'm satisfied," he said with a snarl. "Let's go." He turned on his heel and stomped out of the room, leaving a confused Sam to follow.

Jake was silent on the return to the office and Sam, sensing he was in a foul mood and that she had put him there, didn't attempt to speak. He dropped her off at her car, gave a curt "good night," and then drove off without saying another word.

Forty minutes later, Sam was frowning as she bent to retrieve some paper from the front lawn of her townhouse. The fact that rebuffing Jake's advances had resulted in his behaving like a scorned and disgruntled lover troubled her as much as his openly stating there was an attraction between them and urging her to admit it. She didn't want to admit the attraction, primarily because she was loathe to admit that Jake had the ability to awaken emotions long dormant. How amused Jake would be if he knew she had ended his lovemaking because she feared what she might have done if he had continued.

As she kicked off her high-heeled shoes and removed her coat, she began to think about the encounter with Jake in the bedroom closet. She was remembering his penetrating look, the warmth of his kiss, and pondering his most seductive manner when the telephone rang.

Thinking it was Jake calling to check up on her, Sam didn't answer in her usual cheery manner. She was pleasantly surprised to find herself talking with an old suitor, one of the men whom Jake, just hours before, had dubbed as weak. The fact that the man was calling nearly nine months after their relationship ended surprised Sam. They had seen each other on numerous occasions since then, but neither had tried to re-establish the relationship to the level of intimacy it had once been.

The reason for the call surprised Sam more than the call itself; Michael told her he had just read the announcement of her engagement to Jake Sloan and wanted to say congratulations since he was sure Sam's future husband wouldn't want a former and intimate acquaintance of hers at the wedding. Sam accepted the best wishes because she knew Michael offered them with genuine warmth. She skirted the question of when the wedding was to take place by simply stating it was to occur very soon. Even before she said goodbye, Sam was online, searching for the announcement.

Sam scanned the Web, looking for the picture the photographer had taken that morning. Her search was interrupted by the ringing of the telephone again. This time the caller was someone whom she had neither seen nor heard from in more than sixteen months. The reason for the second call was the same as the first—the conveyance of congratulations. Sam suspected the second caller, a former business associate who she didn't particularly like, to be motivated by curiosity rather than by a sincere desire to extend good wishes. After the second call, she searched more frantically for the picture and was astounded to find the picture and the announcement consumed an entire webpage.

The telephone continued to ring for hours. Even Jill and her grandfather called to comment on the picture. Coincidentally, both shared an opinion that Sam and Jake made an attractive couple, which did not please Sam. Several other callers made similar comments.

Shortly after a call at eleven o'clock, Sam turned off the telephone. As she prepared for bed she wondered why Jake hadn't called, not that she had any real interest in speaking with him. She merely found it odd that he hadn't called given his earlier performance and his royal reprimand for her having been out the previous night.

Much later, as she slid under the down comforter and stretched out on her bed, Sam had a vision of another bed. Jake's bed. The size of the master bedroom at Jake's was not what alarmed Sam; after all, king-size beds were not unique. What she found alarming were the thoughts and the visions the mere sight of the bed had generated. She had actually seen herself lying in the bed with Jake! She had visualized his naked body pressed against hers, one of his arms wrapped possessively around her waist. She shuddered at the memory. Jake Sloan was her enemy, so why was she picturing herself in such an amorous setting with him? Why was she imagining his touch? It simply didn't make any sense for her mind to want one thing and her body to want another.

Although exhausted, Sam was restless. She lay awake for many hours, continuing to try to rationalize the mixed emotions she felt toward Jake. The recollection of one of Jake's statements finally ended her mental tussle. Jake had appeared particularly confident when he had told her, "As your husband, I'll determine how you live."

Even now, hours later, anger swelled within her at the memory. Sam rolled over, punched her pillow until there was a nice comfortable indent, and then burrowed her head into its folds, saying to the ceiling, "That's what you think Jake Sloan!"

Chapter 14

Midweek Sam quit thinking of Saturday as being days away, and started thinking of it as being hours away. Her anxiety level climbed with each passing hour, as did her temper. With her emotions threadbare, encounters with Jake became even more difficult. She became increasingly more obstinate and more argumentative until Jake's patience was exhausted and he told her in no uncertain terms to revise her disposition or he would do it for her. To drive the threat home, he snapped a pencil into two jagged pieces.

In the few private moments available to her and between packing up some particularly fragile personal possessions and selecting a wedding costume—a chore she abhorred—Sam worked out the details of how she was going to escape from Jake. The entire plan revolved around the receipt of the original of her father's letter confessing his part in the death of Jake's father. Jake had promised he would give it to her at the reception and not a minute before. She prayed it was the one promise he had ever made that he would definitely keep.

Friday morning Sam got lucky. Jake telephoned early and announced he was cancelling a scheduled meeting. The news presented her with the first opportunity in days to have some privacy. She closed and locked her office door after telling Karen she didn't want to be disturbed and began executing the plan she had engineered. Her first order of business was to arrange for a rental car, which proved to be an easy task as she had the required major credit card. Fulfilling the second crucial item of her plan proved slightly more difficult. It took no less than ten telephone calls to three different taxi companies before she found a driver who would agree to the arrangement she had laid out. And before he did agree, Sam had to convince him she was not a crackpot and had to promise a hefty cash bonus.

With the exception of one thing, the remaining details of the plan were relatively simple to carry out. The exception was a letter to Jake. Composing a clear, concise, unemotional letter turned out to be the most difficult task of all. She spent hours writing and rewriting it, explaining her feelings, outlining her demands. Once the letter was completed, the plan was complete, and her spirits lifted.

That night, the eve of her wedding, Sam stayed at her grandfather's. She had no choice. Earlier in the afternoon the movers had descended like a swarm of hornets upon her house and packed and transported all of her household goods and personal effects to Jake's. She refused to participate in the merging of her possessions with his, using the excuse that she still had things to do in preparation for the wedding. Jake hadn't been happy about her refusal, but because there was a small audience of men dressed in white overalls, he said nothing; he just glared at her. Sam smiled all the way to her grandfather's.

After settling into a guest bedroom, Sam joined her grandfather for a light supper. As they shared a plate of cold chicken and vegetables, they talked of purely trivial matters like the weather and the economy. It was her grandfather who turned the conversation to the next day's event, a subject she had deliberately avoided talking about since her arrival.

"Tell me, dear," asked her grandfather casually as he reached for a piece of broccoli, "how do you feel know about marrying Jake?"

Sam finished her chicken before answering. "I feel fine." Now that she had an escape plan in motion, it was true. She didn't think of the wedding as being real. Her grandfather's eyebrows raised and he looked at her critically.

Sam, realizing she had made a mistake by responding too calmly to his question, expanded her statement. "Naturally, I have the…you know…the jitters." As evidence, she held out her hand to show him how it twitched, a muscular reaction that she produced voluntarily.

Charles Ward's eyebrows lowered, but a look of skepticism remained. Silent minutes passed as he considered her remarks. Sam's heart was pounding. Finally he reached for a second piece of chicken and said no more on the subject. Sam drew a deep breath, relieved that their conversation on the wedding was over. She hated lying to her grandfather. But there were certain instances, and she considered this to be one, when lies were kinder than truths.

The jitters were real the next morning. As she dressed she told herself there was no reason to be nervous. All she had to do was pretend the wedding was merely a scene in a play, and she and Jake the players. There was no reason, she told her reflection as she stood before a full-length mirror, to work oneself into frenzy. After all, she would be playing the part for a short period. By the end of the day she would be miles away from Jake. She'd be safe.

As Sam struggled to button the back of her dress she wished she had some help. She had politely declined Jill's offer of assistance for the same reason the night before she had declined an invitation to breakfast with her grandfather. She was afraid she would give herself away, would appear too calm and, therefore, raise suspicions and questions. She couldn't afford either. If her grandfather asked questions, so would Jake.

Sam heard a car pull into the driveway and guessed that Jill and John Simms had arrived. Her heart beat a little faster. Their arrival meant the hour of the wedding was drawing closer. She took one last look at herself in the mirror and was stunned by her own reflection. The elegant, knee-length crème-colored silk dress purchased at an exclusive designer shop was not supposed to look like a bridal gown, but it did. With matching shoes and a short, lace veil she looked like a bride. Sam sighed heavily as she put on pearl earrings, the only jewelry besides her engagement ring she intended to wear. She braced herself, pressed a hand to her stomach to still the butterflies, and opened the bedroom door.

When she descended the stairs, she found her grandfather and the Simms standing in the foyer, engaged in animated conversation. Her grandfather was the first to see her. He smiled warmly and said with unmistakable pride, "Samantha, you're a beautiful bride."

Jill turned, clapped her hands together, and cried with delight, "Oh, Sam, you do look beautiful."

"Beautiful," piped up John with a squeak and everybody laughed.

The moment of frivolity was cut short by the ringing of the telephone. Her grandfather answered it and she heard him say, "Yes, we're ready here, Jake. We'll see you in twenty minutes."

Twenty minutes! Panic gripped her. Within an hour she would be Mrs. Jake Sloan. She turned her head away, but not before Jill saw the change in her facial expression.

"Sam, what's wrong?" Three pairs of eyes were upon her.

Disguising the real reason for her dismay, Sam cried, "My bag. I've forgotten my bag." The bag was important and she'd forgotten it. It contained clothes and money and keys needed for her escape.

"Is that all!" complained Jill. "For a minute there I thought...well, never mind. Don't worry. John will fetch it for you. Where is it?"

"Second bedroom on the right."

While John went to retrieve the bag, her grandfather went to get her bridal bouquet, leaving Sam and Jill alone.

Jill glanced over her shoulder to make sure they were alone. "Are you okay?" Her beautifully arched brows were furrowed in concern. "For a minute there I thought you were going to announce that the wedding was off!"

Sam laughed nervously, "Call it off? After spending a small fortune on this dress? Don't be silly!"

Jill laughed. "Incidentally, it's tradition for the bride to receive something old, something new, something borrowed, and something blue. I brought the something blue." Jill reached into her purse and pulled out an inch-wide, elasticized blue garter trimmed with frilly white lace.

Sam took the satin article from Jill with a giggle and went into the bathroom to put it on. She came out saying, "Don't you dare tell anyone I'm wearing a garter! I have no intention of letting Jake remove it...in public." She had no intention of letting him remove it at all!

"Let Jake remove what?" asked her grandfather, carrying her flower bouquet in one hand and a small paper bag in the other. John had returned with her bag.

"Nothing. Jill just gave me something blue." She took the small nosegay of pink rosebuds and Baby's Breath from him. "What's in the paper bag?"

There was a twinkle in Charles Ward's eye. "The something borrowed, something old, and something new. The borrowed is a bracelet that belonged to your grandmother." He handed the bag to Jill, told her not to peek, and extracted a fine gold bracelet and clasped it on Sam's wrist. Sam recognized the bracelet; her grandmother had always worn it on special occasions. She knew it was the first piece of jewelry Charles Ward had given to his wife. The gesture touched her. Even Jill appeared emotional.

"The old is a lace handkerchief your grandmother and mother carried when they were married. I'd like you to have it."

Sam's eyes misted as she accepted the delicate piece of ivory lace and linen.

"And now, Sam, the something new." He handed her a large, square, blue velvet case. Sam looked at her grandfather and then at the case. It was obviously jewelry. She opened it and gasped. Lying on a bed of ivory silk was an exquisite strand of perfectly matched cultured pearls.

"Granddad, they're beautiful," exclaimed Sam, her hand at her throat.

She fumbled with the gold clasp studded with tiny seed pearls and her grandfather covered her hands with his and said huskily, "Please. I'd like to have the pleasure of putting them on my granddaughter on her wedding day."

Sam lifted her hair while he secured the clasp. She turned and hugged him tightly, then kissed his cheek and whispered in his ear, "I love you, Granddad."

She heard a sniffle from Jill. Her grandfather pulled away and brushed a hand across his eyes. "Well, now," he said, his voice not quite normal, "you're going to be late for your own wedding if we don't hurry. John, do you have the ring?"

John, who had been standing silently at the edge of the group, stepped forward and patted his vest pocket. "Right here."

"Sam, do you have Jake's ring?"

John spoke again. "I have that, too."

"All right then," he grinned. "Let's go to a wedding."

An hour later the ceremony was over and she was Mrs. Jake Sloan. There was an awkward moment during the ceremony when she had stammered over the words "...love, honor, and obey," and again when Jake lifted the ivory veil to kiss her after the justice of the peace pronounced them husband and wife. She had turned her cheek to receive the customary kiss, but he maneuvered her into a position where she was forced to offer him her lips. The kiss, demanding and searching, was embarrassingly long. Only Jake's hold on her free hand had prevented her from wiping her mouth afterward.

Witnesses to the ceremony—the Simms, her grandfather, and a handful of photographers with their noses pressed to the door of the courtroom—extended hearty congratulations as Jake escorted her to his car. Driving through the city, Samantha kept pulling at the narrow wedding band Jake had placed on her finger, twisting and turning it, wishing she could toss it into a gutter. To her, the gold band was not a symbolic circle of love, but Jake Sloan's brand, proclaiming to all that she belonged to him alone.

Her nervous action did not escape Jake's notice. "You'll get used to it Sam, I promise."

"I'll never get used to it. I'll never get used to you." The words tumbled out of her mouth.

The car shot forward as Jake pressed the gas pedal down harder. Sam jerked forward and put a hand on the dashboard to brace herself.

Jake's eyes left the road momentarily and flashed at her. "Married for less than twenty minutes and already picking a fight with your husband." He made a clucking sound with his tongue that produced a tch, tch. "I'm surprised at you, Sam. And I'm not in the mood for surprises. Not today."

Sam cursed herself for her stupidity. Why couldn't she have kept quiet! She couldn't afford to anger Jake today. At least not until later. Not until she had her father's letter. She turned towards Jake, eyes downcast, and said with a measure of humility, "I'm sorry."

The simple apology appeared to appease Jake. The car slowed and she saw him relax his grip on the steering wheel. She was wondering if now was a good time to ask about the letter when they drove through the iron gates of the Bellevue Sporting Club.

Jake parked the car at the entrance to the club. A uniformed attendant took the car keys from Jake as he opened the passenger door. Jake helped Sam out of the car, and then looped her arm through his. Before he could move away, Sam clutched his forearm fiercely, asking in a hushed tone, "When do I get the letter?"

Jake's brows drew together in a frown, "I said you'll have it and you will."

Pushing the matter, "When?"

Jake reached into his Jacket and pulled out a white envelope. "Here." He slapped it into her hand. "Here's your precious letter."

Sam gripped it tightly. She wanted to rip the envelope open to ensure it was indeed her father's original letter, but a sixth sense told her it wasn't an appropriate time.

On impulse, Sam gave the letter back to Jake, "I haven't got anywhere to put it. Why don't you hold onto it until we're ready to leave the reception?" Jake would never know what effort it was for her to relinquish the letter into his keeping!

The action clearly surprised Jake, who took the envelope back with a skeptical look. "You're sure?"

"I'm sure," responded Sam with false gaiety. If nothing else, her action gave Jake the idea that all was well.

Their entrance was greeted with cheers and a hail of good wishes from a throng of guests, most of whom were strangers to Sam. As they weaved their way through the crowd, Sam recognized several Syntronics employees. Jake had invited the more senior employees who shared more than a business acquaintance with the Ward family.

To their guests, Jake and Sam appeared to be the model bride and groom. They drank, ate, danced; posed for pictures; and smiled benevolently at each other. As the third hour of the reception approached Sam was growing wearier, not only because of her participation in the traditional activities, but also because Jake hovered over her like a captivated lover.

His eyes were constantly upon her, his hands never far away from hers. It was more attention than Sam was accustomed to. She had been able to leave Jake's side only once, and that was to powder her nose. By the time the hour for their departure arrived, she was exhausted.

Sam was unusually emotional when making her good-byes to her grandfather and the Simms. Because there were so many onlookers to the farewell, Sam fought back the tears. Sam would have kept them in check if her grandfather hadn't hugged her and told her he loved her and that he would never be far away. She already felt a great distance between them because she was no longer just his granddaughter, but his married granddaughter.

Chapter 15

Mr. and Mrs. Jake Sloan departed the club in a hail of good wishes. The newlyweds were headed for Jake's house. Because of the SALCOMP project, there would be no honeymoon, which didn't disturb Sam in the least. Jake's plans called for something entirely different. At her feet was the bag that contained her clothes for the cabin and her father's letter. Jake had given it to her just before they had said their good-byes. She had taken just enough time to visit the powder room and verify the letter was her father's original before Jake whisked her away. She was still amazed at how easy it had been to get the letter away from Jake.

It was difficult for Sam to maintain a façade of perfect composure as they journeyed to Jake's. The palms of her hands were moist, her throat dry. Her escape was at hand and her stomach was in knots. Every so often she'd glance furtively at Jake to ensure she wasn't giving herself away. She was grateful that Jake was quiet. Normal conversation was beyond her capability at the moment.

When Jake turned the car into the driveway she craned her head sideways and could just make out the tailgate of a vehicle parked off the road just a few hundred yards away. She knew it was the cab waiting for her and her blood pumped a bit faster.

Jake walked a little behind her as she climbed the stairs to the second floor. She made directly for what was now her bathroom and set the bag she carried on the floor. Wiping her hands on a towel, she turned and went to stand by the doorway of the walk-in closet. Aware that Jake was observing her actions, she paused to tell him she was going to change.

He had already removed his suit jacket and was loosening his tie. "Fine," he said with a smile. "I'm going to shower first and then put on something casual. I thought we'd go for a sail this evening and then dine out."

Sam muttered okay and then made a show of searching the closet for an outfit to wear. Jake was still standing near the bed when she closed the bathroom door.

Once inside, she pressed her ear to the door, straining to hear the running water to make sure he was in his bathroom. Very faintly she heard the splashing of water. As quietly as she could, she opened the door a crack to see if his bathroom door was closed. It was. With nervous fingers, Sam undid the buttons of her bridal dress. After kicking off the high heels and hanging up the dress, she slipped into jeans, a half-zip top, pulled on boots, and grabbed a heavy jacket. She opened the bag and withdrew the letter she had written to Jake. She took a deep breath and opened the door. The shower on his side was still going as she laid the letter in the very center of the bed and rushed out of the room, sped down the stairs, and dashed out of doors to the waiting cab.

The driver turned, wide-eyed with surprise, as she opened a door and slid into the back seat. "You the lady that called?" he drawled.

A breathless Sam said, "Yes." She hugged a corner of the back seat and turned and looked down the road, half expecting to see Jake rushing after her.

"Where to?" asked the driver as her put the car in gear.

Sam told him and asked him to hurry. She gave a sigh of relief as the distance separating the cab and the house grew greater and greater. In no time at all she was paying the driver and searching the bag for the keys to the rental car. As she left Bellevue, she marveled at how easy it had been to escape from Jake. Out on the freeway, she headed toward Snoqualmie and pictured the surprise on Jake's face when he discovered she was gone. A smile touched her lips and then faded as she thought about what would happen if Jake caught up with her. She pushed the horrible scene that filled her mind aside, telling herself that he wasn't going to find her.

It was his fault anyway the she was running away! He was the one who was so...unbendable, inflexible. She didn't want the marriage to be as Jake dictated. He would be overbearing, offensive, insensitive, and unsympathetic in any situation where he believed her to be challenging his authority. She simply couldn't be the docile and obsequious little wife he wanted.

She was going to follow through with her plan just as she had worked it out. She would hide out at the cabin for two days and then would call him, as she said she would in the letter, to find out if he was going to agree to her conditions.

Two days, she hoped, would be sufficient time for Jake to calm down and consider her conditions rationally.

Slowly the tension subsided and she relaxed. Her driving was an execution of long habit more than concentration. In no time at all she found herself pulling into the gravel driveway to the cabin, unlocking the front door, and throwing the bolt behind her.

Sam breathed a sigh of relief when she stepped inside. She had reached sanctuary, and escaped Jake and his domination. But for how long she wondered. Remaining in the cabin was a temporary reprieve, not a permanent solution. She would have to return to Seattle sometime, and return to her work, her grandfather, and, reluctantly, to her husband. She prayed that Jake would be reasonable and they could compromise.

The darkening of the room and the chill beginning to seep through her jacket awakened Sam from her thoughts. She didn't know how long she had been standing with her back against the door, still fully clothed in outdoor wear, still clutching her purse, which had been hidden in the bag, in her right hand, keys in her left. She vaguely remembered it had been daylight when she arrived. It had since faded into twilight and now to night.

Throwing her purse and keys on the kitchen counter, she rummaged through a drawer to find matches to light the fireplace. Within half an hour the chill in the small one-bedroom cabin was burned off. Before long she was in an old plaid shirt of her grandfather's that long ago had been pressed into service as a nightshirt. She settled into an ancient recliner in front of the roaring fire and sipped wine.

As fatigue and the wine took command of her body and mind, Sam rested at last. When the wine was finished, she crawled into bed and fell into a deep sleep.

Hours later she sat up, alert, unsure at first of what had awakened her. Then she remembered that it had been a sound, a loud noise from the only other room in the cabin. She peered through the open doorway of the bedroom, surprised to find that the fire she had started earlier was still blazing. The room was in shadow except for the rippling glow of the fire. The flames cast a muted golden hue over everything.

She was just about to make sure the front and only door to the cabin was secure when she heard another sound. This time she recognized the noise as the loud jangling of keys. Trembling, Sam called out sharply, "Who's there?" and then thought how absurd the question was. There was a quick intake of breath as a familiar voice answered gruffly, "Your husband." And then Jake stepped across the threshold, slammed the front door shut, and crossed the living room in a few strides.

They stared at each other across the expanse of darkness. Neither spoke. When he stepped closer to the bed, she pulled the covers higher, just under her chin. Sam wondered how he had found her so quickly and a single person came to her mind—her grandfather. Learning she had disappeared on her wedding night would have infuriated her grandfather almost as much as it would have infuriated Jake. Only her grandfather would have guessed she would run to the cabin, as she had on previous occasions when faced with a stressful situation. It was the one flaw in her plan she had not anticipated—betrayal.

She saw Jake raise an arm, but at first couldn't tell what he was doing. Then her eyes adjusted to the subdued light and she had her answer. Slowly, methodically, he was undressing. Watching a man undress wasn't exactly a new experience, but there was a significant difference this time—the man was her husband.

Sam watched, almost mesmerized as he unbuttoned one cuff of his shirt and then the other. Next he unbuttoned the shirt itself, slipped out of it with just a few fluid motions and flung it carelessly to the floor. His undershirt followed, revealing a muscular and well-toned upper torso. When his hands fell to his belt buckle Sam swallowed hard and pulled her legs under her. He freed the belt and then reached down and unhooked the single button at the waist of his slacks. Sam's pulse quickened when he undid his zipper and then wrenched his slacks and underwear down in one quick action, bending to free himself from his last article of clothing, his socks. He rose again to his full height, and Sam's heart stopped beating. She couldn't speak any more than she could breathe normally. There was no need to ask what he wanted. She knew what he wanted. He wanted her.

Huddled against the headboard, Sam waited for his next move, afraid to speak. When he placed his hands on the very edge of the bed, she pressed all the harder against the headboard. Jake's hands tightened around the blanket and he ripped it from her grasp and off the bed in one quick, furious motion. Sam screamed, surprised by his action and frightened by the fury she saw in his face. Her throat was dry. Her heart was pounding so hard she thought it would burst.

When he eased one knee on to the bed and then another, the bed creaked under his weight. He then crawled toward her, his eyes never once leaving her face. Having seen the cold rage that motivated his actions, Sam was panic-stricken. She extended both hands to ward him off, saying huskily, "Jake, please don't." The plea didn't stop him. As he hovered over her Sam reached out and pushed with all her strength against his bare shoulders, beseeching him to stop. In answer he snatched her nightshirt just above each breast and roughly pulled her under him, then wrapped his hands around her wrists and pinned her arms above her head.

When he tore open the nightshirt and ran a hand gently across her breasts she tried to twist away from him, but the violent thrashing of her body only served to excite him. He began tracing a pattern across her belly, his long slender fingers like tiny feathers making her body tingle. As his hand plunged lower still and found the spot it sought, she could hold back no longer and moaned in response to the sensations he was creating. He gave a low chuckle and Sam cursed him. His hand traveled down her left leg and then stopped at her knee. Suddenly he pushed her leg upward, bending it, pressing it against her torso and then inched his body forward, adjusting it to fit hers. Lying crushed beneath his body, feeling the long hard evidence of his arousal burning into her thigh; she closed her eyes and turned her face to one side. She knew Jake was not going to be gentle. There was nothing she could do, nothing she could say, to dissuade him from his purpose, and she wasn't even sure if she wanted to. Just before he laid total claim to her body she heard him say, "You're mine."

CHAPTER 16

To her relief Jake was gone from the bed when she woke the next morning. She winced as she stretched awake. Her body still ached from his lovemaking. She closed her eyes tightly against the memory of his utter possession of her. At first, with his fury hot and consumed by a harsh urgency to punish her, his lovemaking had been tumultuous, leaving her body bruised and quaking. But then, the anger turned to desire, the harshness to gentleness, and he became an ardent lover who beckoned her with every movement of his taut, virile body, to answer his needs with her own. Under his seductive possession, she had given way, had whispered her desires, had called his name, and begged him not to stop.

Her emotions were a mixture of shame and embarrassment as she recalled the wildness of their unions. How was she going to face Jake! With a moan she turned over and wrapped the tangled sheet about her. She rolled out of bed and raced to the bathroom, locking the door behind her. She showered and dressed quickly. When she opened the door, Jake, his eyes shining brightly, his face set grimly, was sitting on the bed. She blushed under his intent gaze and walked by him stiffly.

She was near the bedroom door, about to enter the living room, when he spoke.

"Give me the keys, Sam." The words were flat, mechanical, cold.

She twisted her head around, talking over her shoulder. "Keys? What keys?"

"The rental car keys, the cabin keys. All your keys." He stood then, his hands on hips, his eyes narrowed.

"Why?" she crossed her arms as if to ward off the anger emanating from him and leaned against the door jam.

"Just give me the keys," He snapped. "Now."

Sam gave him a contemptuous look and received one in return. Confiscating her keys equated to imprisonment. "But I need my keys."

"I said now!" He thundered. He stepped toward her threateningly and she dashed out of reach. He followed her into the kitchen, where she found her purse and keys on the counter. She snatched up the keys, only to have them torn from her grasp.

Upset by this new development, she stammered "Ja...Jake...I can understand..."

"You understand nothing!" He said savagely. The keys were buried in his pocket.

"I have to have my own transportation." She bit her lip. She had owned her own car since she was sixteen. The idea of having to rely on someone else to chauffeur her about was ludicrous.

"You'll have exactly what I say you can have."

"But..."

"No buts, Sam. Get your things together, we're going home."

Home. God, she wished she could go home. To her home, not to his prison. Her bottom lip was trembling as she told him, "I don't want to go."

He moved his face so close to hers she could see the tiny flecks of grey, like cold ash, in his eyes. "I don't give a damn what you want. You're going."

"Why can't you leave me alone! I married you. Isn't that enough?"

"You becoming my wife hardly compensates me for the death of my father, the ruination of my family name, or the suffering my mother has endured. Nor does having control of Syntronics lessen the vengeance I want."

Now the truth was out. His intent was clear. "What you really want is to punish me at every opportunity! To humiliate me, intimidate me, control me," Sam shouted.

"That's right," Jake said with a smirk.

She glared at him, felt the stiffening of her neck, her right hand twitched. She wanted desperately to slap his face, to hurt him as he was hurting her.

"Careful, Sam," he cautioned, watching the thoughts play across her face. "I slap back."

It was a challenge Sam couldn't ignore. Even as her hand made the descending arc, she knew she would regret the action, but she hit him nevertheless and the blow left her hand stinging. In response, Jake reached for her, his hands biting into her upper arms, and flung her across his knee. He administered several hard, painful slaps to her back end before standing her roughly upright. Instinctively, she turned to run, bent on escape, hot tears of humiliation running down her cheeks. Her flight to freedom was stopped as her upper arms were again gripped tightly from behind.

"Let me go," she screamed as she tried frantically to pull away. His answer was to draw her back tightly against his chest. Sam felt his hot breath against her ear, heard him say no as he turned her roughly to face him.

"Listen green eyes," he said slowly. "You can make it easy, or you can make it hard, but you're not going to change the fact that I'm always going to win and you're always going to lose."

Through clenched teeth, Sam spat out a particularly crude obscenity. Jake responded by pushing her into a chair and throwing a warning finger in her face.

"Sam," he snarled. "You're close to pushing me past my limit. One way or another you're going to learn that I'm your master. I'm not going to put up with your vulgar mouth, or your behavior. Now get your things, we're going home!" He threw her purse at her and marched into the bedroom, coming out with the open bag in his hand.

"Get in the car," he said, stuffing the nightshirt she had worn the night before into the bag. He shoved the bag at her and Sam zipped it shut. She walked rapidly to the car, as if the devils of hell were at her heels.

"The rental car," she said. "I need to take it back."

"No, you don't," Jake answered. "I'll take care of it. Now get in the damn car."

All the way home, Jake's hands clenched and unclenched on the steering wheel, a sure sign that he was still furious. Twice she opened her mouth to say something, only getting out a nearly guttural sound. Both times Jake growled for her to keep quiet. Not until they were inside the house did she try to approach him again.

They were in the bedroom. Jake was standing on one side of the bed, she on the other. Setting her bag on the bed, playing with the strap, Sam took a deep breath and said, "Jake, can't we talk about this. I know you're…angry…livid with me because I ran away, but if you'd just try to understand…" Her voice trailed off as she looked up. Jake wasn't listening to her. He wasn't even in the room. Feeling completely defeated, she sat down on the bed, covered her face with her hands, and sobbed.

Sometime later she got up and went into the bathroom to wash her face. When she came out, Jake was standing in the room in much the same spot as he was when she had last seen him. From his aggressive stance, it was plain to see that his disposition toward her hadn't improved. She stood awkwardly before him twisting a tissue between her hands, waiting anxiously for him to end the stifling silence and to open the conversation.

As the minutes ticked by, it became increasingly evident to her that Jake wasn't in any hurry to speak, only to bear witness to her growing unease. The fact that she felt vulnerable added to her discomfort. Jake was so unpredictable and she wasn't sure what he would do next. By now the tissue had been shredded into thin strips. She turned her attention to a loose button on her shirt, nervously twisting it in a circular motion. And still Jake didn't speak. Finally she did, and verbalized the conclusion she had reached after Jake had demanded her keys.

Her voice cracked as she said, "You don't trust me."

"I don't trust you."

"Because I ran away."

"Because you ran away."

Thinking she could explain her actions, she said, "I couldn't—can't—live under your rules."

"So you said," his voice was expressionless. He wasn't making her efforts to explain her behavior any easier.

Frustrated by his pat answers, Sam cried passionately, "Do you understand anything I said, anything I wrote in the letter?"

There was no more emotion in his voice than before. "I understand that you want to continue living the life of a single woman when you're married. I understand you want no responsibility in a relationship other than your immediate wants. I also understand that you expect no consequences for your actions."

His assessment made her seem selfish, self-centered, and spoiled. He was wrong and she told him so.

Sam pouted, "It's not true. How you describe me, I mean."

"I think it is."

"And I think your perspective is subjective."

Jake snorted, and then said, "That's obvious."

Tired of standing, Sam walked over to an easy chair set in the corner, asking as she went, "If you had married under normal circumstances, would you feel and act the same?"

Without any hesitation he answered, "Absolutely."

At first, the admission flabbergasted Sam, but then she realized that his attitudes weren't all that unique. Many men acted one way, but thought another. She would be the first to acknowledge that the personality of this man was complex and confounding. She also knew him to be chauvinistic and slightly machismo. Still, she never expected him to openly admit to her that he possessed these characteristics.

"Don't you think your attitudes are out of place with today's more liberal relationships?"

He gave a single syllable response. "No."

Sam sighed heavily. "I was reared to be independent, not subservient. You can't expect me to let you dominate me!"

"Funny," Jake drawled sarcastically, "from your performance last night I would have said that you thoroughly enjoy being dominated. Or are you one of those women who has one set of rules for the bedroom and another for the boardroom?"

He was throwing her own words back at her. Sam's face colored with embarrassment at his reference to their lovemaking of the previous night. Ignoring his question, she retaliated smartly with, "You practically raped me."

The accusation didn't sit well with Jake. Even from a space of a few feet she could see his jaw shift and tighten. She deliberately looked away.

"Rape?" he scoffed, his eyebrows arched high. "Sam, you're lucky I made love to you instead of giving you the beating you deserved." There was a long pause before he added, "Besides, you were the one who asked for more."

Sam's head jerked up, her eyes flashing. His last statement was meant to cut deep and it did. So much so that she was rendered speechless.

Jake continued his verbal assault. His words were laden with reproach. "Grow up, Sam, and get rid of those juvenile ideas about marriage once and for all. Contrary to your belief, our marriage is not founded upon democratic principles. You don't have a license to do whatever you please, whenever you please. So don't fight me on the issue, because the more you fight the more determined I am to demonstrate to you that I alone rule here. If you get hurt in the process you have no one to blame but yourself."

It would have been prudent to remain silent, but Sam didn't. "You accuse me of having 'juvenile ideas' and then talk about ruling over me as though I was some kind of bonded servant!" Shaking her head, she added, "It's unconscionable to me that an intelligent man can have such archaic beliefs."

He retorted to her recrimination with a scowl and, "Even an intelligent man can be persuaded to alter his beliefs if given sufficient reason, or should I say, provocation."

Not quite sure she was reading him correctly, Sam countered, "Are you implying that I'm responsible for your behavior, your attitudes? Because I won't believe or accept that, not for a moment."

"I'm saying that my attitudes aren't going to change until yours do."

"Why is it that I have to change? Why can't you change? After all, you're the one who insisted on this farcical marriage."

Jake gave a harsh, ugly laugh. "How quickly you've forgotten the reason for my marrying you. You were payment for my silence, remember?"

Sam muttered between tight lips, "I remember."

"I'm so glad you do, wife, because I don't want to have to remind you daily. Just as I don't want to have this conversation again. We've had this conversation several times before. It's growing very boring."

"If you would only compromise, this conversation wouldn't be necessary." Her voice was growing progressively louder, her tone sharper as she spoke.

Sam heard the force behind Jake's next words. "There will be no compromise and you have only yourself to blame. You shouldn't have run away."

She screeched at him then. "I should have run farther!"

"I would have found you and the end result would have been the same. For your own well-being, I suggest you don't try it again." He paused briefly, looked at his watch, then announced, "I have to go out for a while and I expect to find you here when I return. Understand, Sam?"

"Understand, Jake," She answered sharply in a very prim fashion.

"And remember that this," he pointed to the bed, "is where you'll be sleeping."

Sam looked at him with hostile eyes, but said nothing. She remained seated until long after she had heard him drive off. For the remainder of the afternoon, she occupied herself with exploring the house in greater detail and finally went to bed early, bone weary from her experience the night before. She didn't even wake when Jake slid in next to her many hours later.

CHAPTER 17

Sam woke with a start the next morning. The first shock was finding herself in unfamiliar surroundings; the second was finding she wasn't alone. It didn't take long for her to become totally alert and slide closer to the edge of the bed, away from Jake's nude, prone body. In the private minutes she had before he woke, Sam surreptitiously inspected his still form. Until then, she had never known Jake had a diamond-shaped birthmark on the lower part of his left shoulder, a jagged scar above his right elbow, and a cowlick at the crown of his head. Her inspection would have proceeded downward, but Jake woke and found her watching him. He gave her a gravelly "Good morning," and asked if she liked what she saw. She returned the greeting with a brisk, "Good morning," and flew out of bed and ran into her bathroom before Jake could say another word.

By the time she came out, Jake was in his shower. She dressed hurriedly and was slipping on her shoes when he entered the common area of the bedroom, a towel wrapped around his lower torso. She was just about to ask if there was coffee in the kitchen, when Jake smiled at her, whipped the towel off and rambled leisurely into his dressing room. Sam's mouth dropped open in surprise, aghast at his provocative display. Then she realized it was his unique way of telling her it wasn't necessary to sneak peeks at his body while he slept; it was perfectly all right for her to look at any time. She carried the thought into the kitchen as she searched for the coffee. Jake strolled in, adjusting his tie, as she opened the last cupboard. She gazed up at him and said, "I can't find any coffee."

"There isn't any coffee," he told her, opening the refrigerator.

"No coffee?" she asked incredulously.

Pouring a glass of orange juice, he said, "No coffee. I don't drink it. I'll leave a note for the housekeeper to pick up some today. What brand?"

"What housekeeper?" It was news to her that Jake had someone come in, though it was silly that it hadn't occurred to her before. The house was far too tidy to be kept up by a busy man like Jake.

"Mrs. Sally Barnes, a widow with a teenage boy, comes in daily for half days. Sometimes I have her in on weekends, but only on special occasions."

"Oh." It sounded like a perfect arrangement. "So I don't have to worry about any of the housework."

"Nor shopping or preparing meals. Unless, of course, you'd like to do them yourself."

"No. Let's just leave things as they are." She hated housework and she wasn't that keen on cooking daily, though she did like to demonstrate her excellent culinary skills from time to time.

"Make a list today of the foods you like. We'll get together with Sally."

In the next half hour Sam learned about some of Jake's other idiosyncrasies besides not liking coffee. He liked a full breakfast with his toast unbuttered and cut into fingers, his eggs over easy, a half cup of fresh fruit on the side, and the Wall Street Journal on the table. And he liked to eat in silence.

Conversely, she liked a continental breakfast of coffee and buttered toast. The only thing they shared in common for their first meal together as husband and wife was a desire for no conversation.

There was a tense moment shortly after breakfast when they were preparing to leave for the office. Sam boldly asked for her car keys and Jake told her in quick order she wasn't having them for some time. It was too early in the morning to argue the point, so Sam didn't pursue the subject.

It occurred to her as they pulled into the Syntronics parking garage the Jake hadn't mentioned where he'd been last night. She wasn't foolish enough to make the inquiry, lest it be misconstrued as wifely concern instead of what it actually was—idle curiosity. So she kept quiet, deciding to wait and see if he would tell her, though she doubted he would. Answering to his wife, she was sure, was not one of his rules. Besides, she had a more important question to ask. One she was sure Jake would consider trivial, but one she considered important enough to delay their arrival by five minutes. She waited until Jake parked the car and pulled the keys out of the ignition. He sensed her hesitancy on exiting the car and asked what the problem was.

Staring straight ahead, she said, "I have a question to ask you."

"If it's a question we've already covered..." he began harshly and Sam cut him off.

"It's not," she assured him. "I want to know what our relationship is to be at the office. Husband and wife, or employer and employee?"

"Both."

It was the answer Sam expected and dreaded. "That will be difficult. Professionally, I want to continue to be thought of and known as Samantha Ward. If I do and you treat me as your wife, people will get conflicting signals. I don't want that."

Jake drummed a single finger on the steering wheel as he considered her statement. Finally he said, "I have no objection to the professional use of your maiden name. But, I do mean, professionally. In all other areas, especially social, you'll be Mrs. Jake Sloan. Agreed?"

"Agreed. But what about the other?"

"I don't think you'll find that other people will be confused as long as you're not."

At least he agreed to her retaining the name Ward professionally and that was a small point to be grateful for.

Karen was the first to greet them and the first to address them as Mr. and Mrs. Sloan. Sam smiled but told Karen to please continue addressing her as she had before. She and Jake parted at the door to her office.

Mid-morning Jake called Sam to his office. Since he was brusque when he made the request, Sam expected the worst. She marched into his office with a defensive air, coming to an abrupt halt mid-stride, just short of his desk. Jake was sitting behind his desk, jacket and tie removed, shirt rolled up to his elbows. It was the first time Sam saw Jake really at work. Even his desk was untidy; its entire surface was covered with files and odd little piles of handwritten notes. It was an amazing sight.

She could tell from his tone of voice as he directed her to sit that something serious had occurred. She elected not to sit and Jake slammed the pen in his right hand onto the notepad.

"Okay, stand then," he said curtly. "I found out last night that Softpro, Syntronics biggest competitor, is just six months away from releasing a new software package very similar to ours. The accuracy of the information was confirmed just fifteen minutes ago, which is why I didn't mention it to you earlier. I want you to coordinate a meeting for 8 a.m. tomorrow in the conference room. All project personnel are to attend. This afternoon, I want a project progress report from each department head. Just tell them I want the information, but don't tell them why. The fewer people who know about Softpro the better."

Sam stared blankly at Jake, numbed by what could only be called disastrous news. If Softpro's package hit the marketplace before theirs, it would mean an end to Syntronics. Recovering from the shock, she asked, "How did you find this out?"

Jake's answer was ambiguous. "I have a source." He anticipated her next question of "What source?" and responded, "Just someone I do business with. The details don't matter. What does matter is getting into action now. SALCOMP has to be in the marketplace in three weeks."

"All right." Her mind was reeling with the aspects of the projects that remained half finished. "I'll advise the necessary people that a report has to be done. What time do you want the reports on your desk?"

"Four o'clock."

It was nearly noon, she'd have to hurry. "Okay." She turned to leave. "Anything else?"

"We'll have to dine out tonight. I've already called Sally and told her not to prepare anything."

"Fine," mumbled Sam, not really caring. She sped out of the office. Because it was nearly the lunch hour, she had to race to catch all the department heads. Each wanted to know what the urgency was. Sam merely shrugged her shoulders in answer.

A stack of reports were handed to Jake at four sharp. Sam delivered them personally. As Jake finished reading a report, she would pick it up and read it. An hour later Jake proclaimed that SALCOMP, with a little team effort and a lot of hard work, could definitely be ready for marketing in three weeks. The news seemed to relieve Jake as much as it relieved her.

Adjusting his tie, Jake said, "I've finished everything I need to for the meeting tomorrow morning. How about you?" Sam told him she was ready.

"I bet you didn't have lunch either." Commented Jake as he rolled down his shirt sleeves.

"No, I didn't." After hearing the news about Softpro, Sam had been unable to eat.

"Are you hungry?"

"Umm, not particularly." She felt the tug of an empty stomach and revised her answer. "Well, a salad would be nice."

"Well, I'm ravenous. And I know just the place to satisfy my appetite and your desire for a salad."

The place he had in mind turned out to be on the north shore of Lake Washington, a good thirty minute drive from the office. By the time they finished dinner and arrived home, it was eleven o'clock. Still uncomfortable about undressing in front of Jake, Sam changed in the bathroom, putting on her most concealing gown. She was apprehensive as she crawled between the sheets on her side of the bed. Jake had left her alone the previous night, but she wasn't sure if that would be the case tonight.

Her back was to Jake when he came to bed. She lay rigid, pretending to be asleep, silently hoping he would go to sleep. Luck wasn't with her. Jake's arm reached out and circled her waist. He pulled her body towards him until she was pressed tightly against him.

"I know you're not asleep," he murmured in her ear. "Your body is as stiff as a board." His hand slowly moved down her side, exploring the outline of her body.

"No," whispered Sam, "I'm not asleep, but I'm tired, Jake. And tomorrow is going to be a long day."

He nuzzled her neck and stroked her hair. "All I want is a good night kiss from my wife."

Sam was already beginning to feel a warm tingling feeling from his caresses. Reluctantly, she turned over and faced Jake. They were almost nose to nose. The arm around her waist slowly inched upwards. With the tips of his fingers he traced a line along the lace edge of her nightgown just below her shoulder blades and her body automatically began to arch at his sensual touch. He lifted his head, placed a hand gently against her cheek, and lowered his lips to hers.

The kiss, warm and loving, was followed by another and then another, until they were locked in a passionate embrace. Aroused, but still afraid of the sensations and feelings Jake's touch spawned, Sam started to protest. Jake simply kissed her, said "Hush," and then proved to her again that for all the differences between them, sex wasn't one.

Chapter 18

The conference room of Syntronics was the center of activity the next morning. Behind closed doors, Jake told the small assembly that it was absolutely critical the SALCOMP project be in the marketplace in exactly three weeks if Syntronics was to continue. Success, he told them, pretty much depended on their efforts alone. Jake impressed upon them that the survival of Syntronics—their very livelihood—was virtually in their own hands. His announcement resulted in an explosion of questions, most of which were laced with hostility. Only Sam and John Simms sat silently, since neither was surprised by the news. Everyone talking at once caused quite a commotion, and the din in the room rose to a deafening level. Finally, Jake motioned for everyone to be quiet and he calmly took control of the meeting.

He began talking about the SALCOMP project summarizing project progress to date. He followed with a precise accounting of what work remained to be done on the project, highlighting problem areas and soliciting possible suggestions from everyone. Slowly, the group quit functioning as individuals and began operating as a team. Somehow, the problem areas were resolved and resolutions made by all to meet the three-week deadline.

Four hours after the meeting had started it broke up, but not before Jake had mapped out his marketing strategy and short-range plans and long-term goals for Syntronics. Everyone greeted his plans with enthusiasm, including Sam. As people exited and rushed to return to work, Sam felt a swell of pride for Jake's accomplishments. He had deftly disposed of some extremely troubled areas of the project and had made every member of the project feel like they were an important, integral part to the success of the project. By the time she left the meeting, she had a new respect for Jake.

The end of the meeting marked the beginning of three weeks of arduous work. There was a new unity among the employees of Syntronics, a new dedication to surpass the best in the industry by being better.

During that time, Sam saw Jake in a new light. Slowly, subtly, their relationship changed. Jake had begun to trust her and she him. They continued to commute to and from work together, but Jake had, on his own initiative, restored her keys and transportation to her. Though he still policed her activities, she had come to realize his motivation for this was not a hankering to have control over her life, but jealously. The realization rocked her, the depth of which she was unsure.

She was just as unsure about her feelings for him. And, she was afraid to express the feelings she did have. Sometimes, when she lay in his arms or sat across the room from him, sometimes quietly reading while he worked, she felt a wonderful peace within herself and within him. She felt a bond between them—a bond that was more than mere sexual attraction. If Jake felt it, too, he never said, and she couldn't bring herself to ask.

Their days, and most nights, were filled with the SALCOMP project. They rose early every morning and literally fell into bed late each night, exhausted by the grueling pace of the work. After two weeks of this uninterrupted routine, Jake insisted they take time for some social activity and recreation. This consisted of a Friday evening dinner with the Simms, a Saturday afternoon sailing on Lake Washington, and a mid-week concert at the Seattle Center. On each occasion, Sam discovered something new about Jake and found him to be a considerate, pleasant, and enjoyable companion.

By the end of the third week, SALCOMP was packaged and ready for distribution. The advertising campaign hit the television, newspapers, online sites, and magazines the same day the project was released in stores. The first week of sales reached a level beyond their greatest expectations and Syntronics buzzed with excitement. But Jake, being conservative, wanted to suspend any celebrations for at least two months more, "Just to ensure sales maintain at their current level."

What with one thing and another, it turned out to be two and a half months before there was a celebration. On Monday, Jake circulated that there was to be a barbecue at his home this coming Saturday. It was about the same time that Sam began feeling fatigued and ill. Her first thought was she had been overworking and had neglected her health. But she wanted assurances that there was nothing significantly wrong with her so she made an appointment to see the doctor who had administered to her aches and assorted complaints since early childhood.

Old Dr. Smith sat quietly and listened patiently to her symptoms and then performed a series of medical tests, some of which, he told her, he wouldn't have results for until the next day. Sam had left his office confident the cure to her problem was less stress and more rest.

The next afternoon, the doctor called. Sam couldn't mistake the cheeriness in his voice and expected to hear confirmation of her self-diagnosis.

"My dear, I have the test results in and I'm happy to tell you that there's nothing wrong. Nothing that nine months won't cure."

Baffled, Sam repeated, "Nine months?"

There was a chuckle from the other end of the telephone. "You're pregnant, Sam. Congratulations!"

A lump lodged in Sam's throat. She was pregnant? She couldn't be pregnant. How could she be pregnant? She took precautions and was always so careful. When could she have…and then she remembered—her wedding night! How could she have been so stupid?

Caught up with these thoughts, she had forgotten about Dr. Smith. She made a hasty apology. "Forgive me. I didn't mean to keep you hanging. I just…drifted off for a moment. It's such…unexpected news."

"I bet Jake will be delighted," commented the doctor. "We need to start seeing you regularly beginning a month from now. Your mother didn't have any problems with her pregnancy, so I don't think you will either. You're a strong, healthy girl, but start getting plenty of rest, eat properly, and exercise. That's my prescription for the next month. I'll have to refer you to another doctor after your next visit. My baby delivery days are long over."

Sam only half listened to him, still shocked by the news. She was aware that he had finished speaking and managed to say, "Fine."

She was in a daze for the remainder of the day. Fortunately, Jake was preoccupied with meetings until late that night, so she would have time to think about what she was going to do. An old wife's tale sprung to mind, and Sam rushed to the nearest mirror to see if she looked differently, having heard that pregnant women have a certain glow. As far as she could tell, she looked the same, which was a blessing, because she didn't want Jake to guess she was pregnant—not until she figured out exactly how she felt about him, about their marriage.

Turbulent thoughts plagued her. Questions crowded her mind, and behind them, fear. She and Jake had been getting along famously for weeks, but how long would the calm last before another storm? Besides, did she want Jake's child? Did Jake want a child? He certainly never said he did. More importantly, could she sacrifice her career, put aside her ambitions, for motherhood? And if she did, would she be able to continue working after she gave birth?

The internal turmoil pushed into her dreams that night. She saw herself in two scenarios. In the first she was single, living a carefree existence. She saw herself climbing to the top of her field, receiving awards and acclaim for her accomplishments. The second scenario was horrifying.

She saw herself vividly, quite literally chained to Jake with heavy shackles, her hands covering her ears to shut out the shrill and incessant screams of an infant. At the end of the dream, she was gasping for air and grasping for freedom. Her thrashing woke Jake. She succeeded in halting his inquisitiveness by saying she had eaten too much that evening. She lay awake for hours, haunted by the problem.

She still hadn't reached a decision by the time Saturday rolled around because she hadn't been able to come to terms with her feelings for Jake. So far, Jake was unaware of her morning sickness, so she could delay telling him the news for a while, but not indefinitely.

Because Jill was arriving early to help with preparations for the afternoon's festivities, Sam rose before Jake. She was standing outside on the balcony, marveling over the beauty of the morning and enjoying her first cup of coffee, when Jill arrived.

"Good morning," Jill yelled at her from below. "Can you believe this weather? It's going to be a beautiful day for a barbecue." They were blessed with blue skies and a blazing sun.

"I'll be right down to let you in," Sam shouted back and rushed to close their bedroom door because Jake was still sleeping.

Jill sat a brown paper grocery bag on the counter of the downstairs kitchen and started pulling out bottles of catsup, mustard, and jars of assorted pickles and relishes. "Did you get the ingredients to make the dips?" she asked Sam as she folded the bag.

"In the refrigerator to you left, second shelf." Sam was setting up mixing bowls. "Grab the Lea & Perrins sauce, too. I need a drop of it for the crab dip."

"Yuck," Jill wrinkled her nose. "How can people eat something that lives in a shell?"

"Easy," Sam said, opening the container of crab meat she had purchased at the local market. "Just don't think about the shell." She picked up a lump of crab, popped it in her mouth, and giggled when Jill grimaced.

"I'll mix the onion dip," proclaimed Jill. "And, I'll cut up the vegetables. Just keep that crab away from me!"

"Do you want some coffee? I have a fresh pot upstairs."

Jill thought about it for a moment and then shook her head no. "Better not. I had my quota this morning. Maybe later."

Sam was giving one last stir to her crab dip when the queasiness struck. The spoon she was holding dropped to the counter with a clatter. She cupped a hand over her mouth and brushed by Jill to reach the bathroom. Ten minutes later she was feeling better.

Jill was resting against the counter, arms crossed, a deep frown creasing her forehead. "Are you okay?"

"Yes." Sam didn't want to go into any details.

Jill gave Sam one of her you-can't-fool-me-looks and said, "My, God." Then asked, "Does he know?"

Sam sighed. "No."

"Are you going to tell him?"

"I haven't decided yet." She resumed mixing the dip.

"Don't you think he has a right to know?"

"I haven't decided that yet either."

"He's not going to be happy about your keeping the news from him."

Sam stopped what she was doing and stared at Jill. "I don't want him to know yet, Jill. I have some things to think about. So please, don't say anything. Not even to John."

Jill took the rebuke gracefully, but still had to make a comment. "I won't say anything, Sam, but you can't hide the news forever."

"I don't intend to. I just need a little time."

"Time for what," called Jake from the doorway and Sam almost fainted. Jake looked from one to the other.

Jill tried her best to cover for Sam. "Just time to get the dips ready."

Sam saw Jake's expression, knew he didn't believe Jill, and tried to reinforce Jill's statement. "I'm having trouble with the crab dip. Jill suggested I throw it away. Taste it for me, will you?"

Jake took the spoon she offered. "Tastes great to me."

"See Jill," chided Sam. "It's only you."

Jill lifted a single shoulder in a half shrug. "Peasant tastes!"

The insult drew a chuckle from Jake. He told them he needed to get busy with the grills and departed. They waited a full five minutes after he left before talking again. Each eyed the other.

Sam waved a wooden spoon at Jill. "That was too close."

Jill threw a hand to her breast. "Hey, don't blame me. You were the one talking."

"Okay, you're right. But don't bring the subject up again today. Please." She ran a hand through her hair. "You have no idea what my husband is like when he's angry."

"That's the first time I've heard you call Jake that."

"Call him what?" She had started helping Jill cut up vegetables and separated broccoli.

Neatly slicing a cucumber, Jill said, "Your husband."

Sam paused. When had she started thinking of him as her husband? Somehow it seemed perfectly natural—right—to call him that and the revelation came as a mild shock.

Jill jarred her from her thoughts with a lightly delivered admonishment. "You're falling behind. There's another bag of vegetables to be cut up." Sam called her a miserable slave driver and reached for another pile of vegetables.

Jake had spared no expense for the barbecue. Typical barbecue fare like hamburgers, hot dogs, chicken and ribs were in abundance. Games were set up for children and adults alike. The celebration lasted nearly five hours. When the last employee left, Jake, Sam, and John and Jill were in lounge chairs, watching the sunset.

"Great party," said John from behind dark shades.

"It sure was," agreed Jill enthusiastically. "Let's keep it going."

"What do you mean, 'let's keep it going'?" groaned Sam, who felt weak from playing volleyball and chasing after toddlers all afternoon. She looked over at Jake, in a chaise lounge beside her, to see if he was listening. He appeared to be asleep. She was glad. Throughout the day she had caught him looking at her, as if he was trying to figure something out. She was terribly afraid he had heard more than he was saying about her and Jill's earlier conversation.

"Let's go dancing." Jill stood and did a two-step before them.

No one seemed particularly thrilled with the idea. Jill bent and nudged Sam on the shoulder. "Don't be a spoilsport. It'll be fun."

Sam thought a hot bath and bed would be more fun. "I don't know, Jill."

"It's been ages since we went dancing," Jill complained. "Ask Jake if he wants to go."

Samantha frowned and looked over at Jake. The last time she danced with Jake was at their wedding, many months before.

Jill, seeing her hesitation, said, "Go on, Sam, ask him."

Sam really didn't want to. Jake deserved to sleep. He had been behind the grill most of the day. She shook him gently. "Jake, are you awake?"

He didn't bother to open his eyes. "I am now. What?"

"Jill thinks we should go dancing."

"Tonight?" he said with clear aversion.

"Yes."

One eye opened. "Do you want to go?"

He was making the decision hers. Sam grimaced, not wanting to make the choice. She glimpsed Jill's eager face. She desperately wanted to say no, but said yes, thinking she could go for an hour or so, plead exhaustion, and leave.

Jake called across to John, who hadn't offered an opinion on the idea, "It looks like we're going dancing." Sam sensed he wasn't at all pleased with the prospect, but it was too late to withdraw.

John, sounding even less excited than Jake, answered, "It sure does."

Jill grabbed her husband's hand and tugged at it. He allowed her to draw him to his feet. She wrapped her arms around his neck and kissed him. "Let's go home, catch an hour of sleep, shower, then meet at the Hilton downtown two hours from now." She looked to Sam for agreement and received a nod of approval.

After the Simms departed, Sam and Jake wandered upstairs to rest. Sam was the first to rise and prepare for the evening. She had to prod Jake to get up. He was so grumpy that she asked, "Why didn't you just say you didn't want to go?"

"You should have known that I didn't want to go," retorted Jake gruffly.

"If you don't want to go that's fine. I'll go alone."

He scowled. "If I don't go, you don't go."

Sam retorted rather frostily. "That's not fair."

"I don't care whether it's fair or not."

"I can't disappoint Jill."

"But you'll disobey your husband!"

"Disobey?" She couldn't believe what he was saying.

"You heard me."

"I just didn't believe what I heard."

Jake gave her a stony look and went to shower, leaving her to wonder what the reason was for his peculiar behavior. The only thing she could think of was that he was overtired.

The shower didn't cool down Jake's mood. During the drive into Seattle both were silent. Trying to pacify him and defuse his bad mood, Sam offered what she considered a very sensible idea. "Why don't I go in and tell Jill and John that we're tired and we're not going to join them?"

"No."

"Jake…" she began wearily.

Annoyed by his cantankerous behavior, Sam demanded, "What is the problem?"

"If you'll be quiet," he said rudely with a look that chilled her, "there won't be a problem."

Sam's mouth clamped shut. It was no use trying to reason with him. Anything she said would just irritate him, and aggravate the situation.

The fun evening Jill anticipated was a disaster from beginning to end. Sam and Jake dance only a few times because the floor was crowded. When they weren't dancing, they were crammed into a corner, sharing a table better suited to two than four. Most of the time Jake refused to participate in the conversation and maintained a sullen silence. It was so unlike Jake to be antisocial that Sam grew concerned and asked him if he felt well. He answered in a biting tone that he felt fine and Sam didn't ask again.

The exchange, though made in subdued tones, was overheard by Jill. She gave Sam a 'what's up' look. Sam answered by rolling her eyes skyward. John finally ended everybody's misery by saying he was tired and that he wanted to go home. Jill objected and John told her firmly they were leaving. It was the first time Sam had seen Jill overruled by her husband. Sam didn't even bother to object, sure Jake would drag her forcibly from the club if she dared.

On the journey home, Jake drove at a maniacal speed. Sam worried about what was going to happen when they did get home. She could feel the anger building in Jake, filling the interior of the car.

Jake opened the door to the house and Sam swept by him, careful to avoid contact. He slammed the door and she turned and said she was going to bed.

"No, you're not," he informed her. "You and I are going to play a little game."

There was an ugly grate to his voice that frightened her. "What game?"

"Truth or consequences. You tell me the truth or you suffer the consequences."

Sam turned around and walked up the stairs as calmly as she was able. "I don't want to play your game, Jake."

He rushed up the stairs and grabbed her arms tightly at the elbows, forcing her to walk backwards into the living room.

"You're playing," he said sternly, directing her to sit. Sam sat and chewed on a thumbnail.

"That's better. Now let's begin. What were you and Jill talking about earlier today?"

She blinked rapidly and looked down at her feet. "We talked about a lot of different things."

"I'll be more specific. What were you and Jill talking about in the kitchen this morning before I came in?"

Sam's heart skipped several beats. "Talking about?"

"Yes, talking," he said impatiently.

Her voice wavered "Just chit chat."

"It was more than chit chat. Much more."

So he had heard, but how much? She tried to lie. "It wasn't."

"Don't lie to me, Sam." The words tumbled out like the roll of thunder and Sam gave an involuntary shudder.

The thought of this moment had given her nightmares for a week. She bit her lower lip. "What makes you think I'm lying?"

"I know you're lying. So just tell me and get it over with." He sat down in the chair across from her, a small end table between them.

"Really," she continued to lie. "There's nothing…nothing to tell."

His fist slammed down on the table and Sam's heart lurched. "You either tell me now or I'll have John get the truth out of Jill. You may think John's a pushover where Jill's concerned, but if his job is on the line he'll get to the truth, even if he has to employ caveman tactics."

"You wouldn't do that."

"I will do it."

She had no doubt he meant it. "All right."

"All right what?"

She stood and walked over to the window. She turned her back to him, leaned heavily on the window sill, and mumbled the answer he sought.

"What did you say?"

"I'm…I'm…," she couldn't even say the word, "pregnant."

An expletive exploded from him. He ran over, twisted her around to face him. "You're pregnant and you weren't going to tell me?" He sounded hurt and Sam hung her head in shame.

She wasn't sure how to tell him what she was feeling, how to make him understand. "I don't know whether or not I want to go through with this pregnancy."

"Just what the hell does that mean?"

She was close to tears. "It means...it means I never meant to marry. I never planned on having children. I was supposed to be..."

"Oh, I see," Jake cut her off, "your precious career will be interrupted. Well, that's easy enough to solve. Effective Monday, you become an ordinary housewife!"

Her head came up and she faced the full force of his wrath. "You can't do that," she cried.

"Yes I can." He let her go and began pacing up and down in front of her. He stopped and pointed a finger at her. "You're going to have our child if I have to lock you in a room for the next nine months."

Her hands flew to her mouth in a prayer-like position. Her eyes implored him to understand. "Jake," she sobbed. "You can't do that."

"I'll do it." He was shaking with anger. "How dare you try to keep this information from me."

Between sobs she cried. "I didn't think you'd care."

"You didn't think I'd care?"

"No, I didn't."

"Of course I care." He grabbed her and pulled her against his chest. "God, Sam, I care. I love you."

The sobs faded into sporadic gulps and then stopped. Sam couldn't believe his words. "You love me?"

"Yes, Sam, I love you." He kissed her forehead. "I love you. I have for a very long time."

She started to cry again. Jake's arms tightened around her.

"Why are you crying?"

"Because...because I love you, too."

He pushed her away from him, held her at arm's length. "Do you mean what you're saying? Do you really love me?"

Sam hugged him to her, rested her head in the crook of his neck. "Yes. I love you. But I'm afraid."

He gently pulled some tendrils of hair away from her face. "Afraid of what?"

"Of losing my identity. Of being just a half instead of a whole. I'm afraid I can't be a wife, a mother, and a career woman all at the same time. I'm afraid you will do as you've threatened to do and lock me away."

Jake pressed a hand to her stomach, "I want our child as much as I wanted you. If you want to continue working, that's fine with me as long as you don't neglect your health. If you like, we'll hire a full-time nanny after he's born so you can continue working."

"He?" She pulled away and looked at him quizzically.

Jake gave her a sheepish look. "Or her. I don't care as long as the child is healthy. As long as you're happy."

"Do you mean that, Jake?" She returned to the comfort of his arms. "Do you really mean it?"

He hugged her tightly. "I really mean it."

She kissed him passionately. "And you really love me?"

"I really love you."
"Prove it."
And he did.

Chapter 19

A year later, Jake and Sam were spending a quiet evening at home, lavishing all their attention on their infant son, Tyler Ward Sloan. Cradling the sleeping baby in her arms, Sam marveled over the resemblance between father and son.

"He certainly is a Sloan in every detail, including his ferocious little temper," remarked Sam in a whisper as she settled more comfortably into the safety of her husband's arms.

Jake smiled and with the back of his fingers, gently stroked the sleeping child's cheek. "He has your eyes, Sam."

The baby stirred in her arms, as if he knew he was being discussed by his two adoring and doting parents. Sam sat perfectly still, waiting to see if Tyler was going to wake. The tiny eyes remained closed in slumber.

Sam laid her head back against her husband's shoulder, turning her head towards him. "He's such a beautiful baby, Jake."

"Like his mother," offered Jake in a hushed tone and dropped his lips to hers.

Sam still found it difficult to believe she could be so happy. It had been quite a year, one that she was sure she would remember for years to come. In twelve short months she had become a wife and a mother, and had found immense satisfaction in both roles.

Shortly after the night she had announced her pregnancy to Jake, she learned her father had gone to see Jake about a week before his death and had told Jake the truth about his own father's death. Jake had explained to her, "Your father came to me and asked me to take over Syntronics because it was in serious trouble, and because he was dying of cancer. Your grandfather knew, but he hadn't yet told your mother about his condition. There was no cure, Sam, and he didn't have long to live."

Sam had looked at Jake, hardly believing what she was hearing.

"Your father even asked me if I still felt something for you. Smart man. I had loved you since you were seventeen. You were a beauty even then, and I had a hard time staying away, especially that night you were so intoxicated, waiting for you to grow up. In fact, your father was planning a small dinner party to bring us together just before he and your mother were killed. Your grandfather knew about everything, but was sworn to secrecy. When your father died, I didn't know what to do. I was certain you wouldn't have anything to do with me, so your grandfather and I decided to, well, give Cupid a little encouragement."

"It was more like a shove," Sam had told him at the time and Jake had agreed it was, but he was glad and apologized for giving her such a rough time.

A little cry from their son brought her back to the present. Both mother and father peered down at their son and gave a soft, "Sshhh."

Jake looked at Sam lovingly and asked, "You don't have any regrets do you, Sam?"

She smiled happily up at him, "No regrets."